SEARCHING FOR A MARLINSPIKE

SARAH HAMPTON

2QT Limited (Publishing)

First edition published 2021
2QT Limited (Publishing)
Settle, North Yorkshire UK

www.2qt.co.uk

Copyright © 2021 Sarah Hampton. All rights reserved.
The right of Sarah Hampton to be identified as the author
of this work has been asserted by her in accordance with the
Copyright, Designs and Patents Act 1988

All rights reserved. This book is sold subject to the condition that no part of this book is to be reproduced, in any shape or form. Or by way of trade, stored in a retrieval system or transmitted in any form or by any means, electronic, mechanical, photocopying, recording, be lent, re-sold, hired out or otherwise circulated in any form of binding or cover other than that in which it is published and without a similar condition, including this condition being imposed on the subsequent purchaser, without prior permission of the copyright holder.

Cover design - Hilary Pitt
Images supplied by Shutterstock.com

Publisher disclaimer
Searching for a Marlinspike is a work of fiction and any resemblance to any person living or dead is purely coincidental.

Printed by IngramSpark UK Ltd

A CIP catalogue record for this book is available
from the British Library
ISBN 978-1-914083-31-0

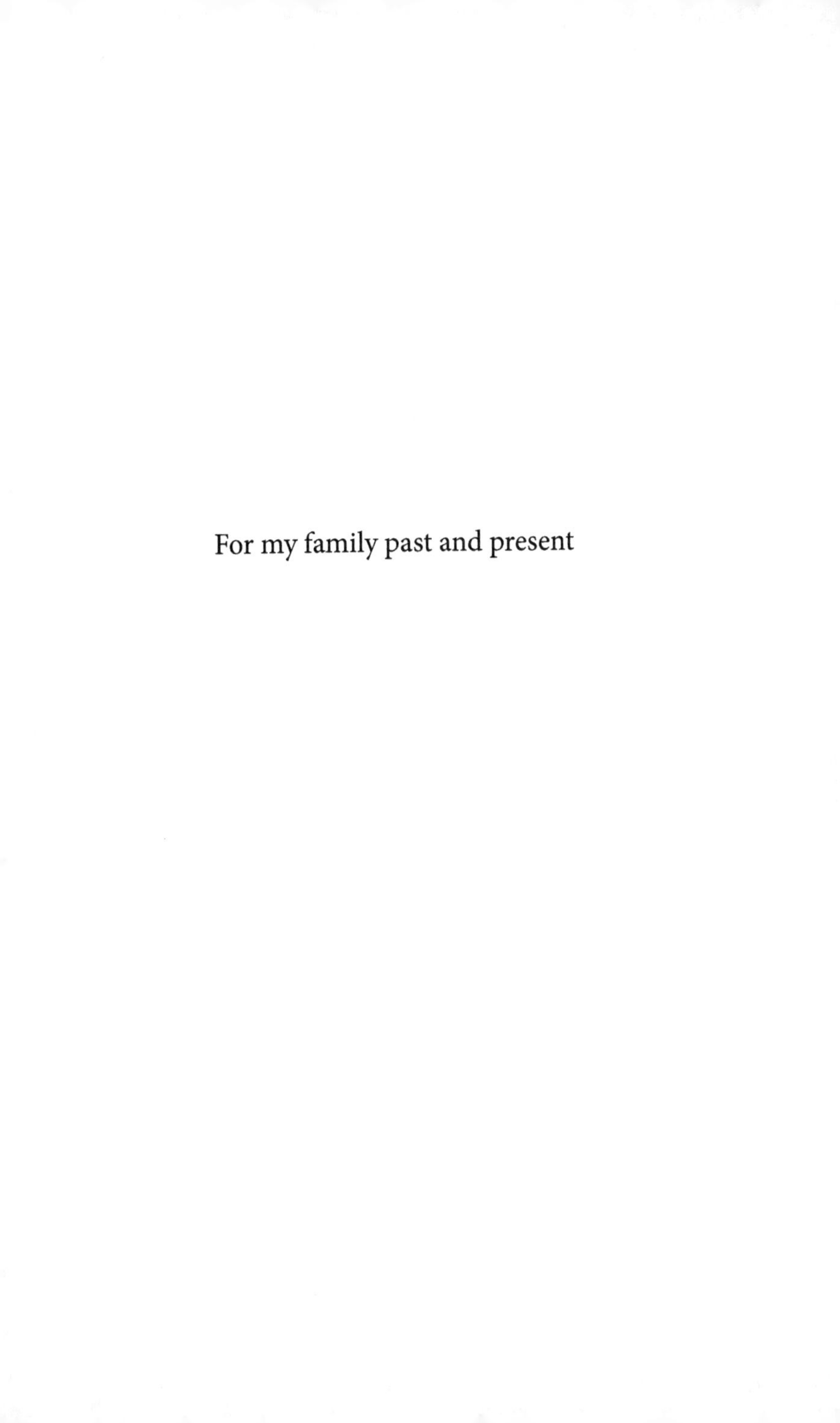

For my family past and present

Other titles by Sarah Hampton

Learning to Tie A Bow
Picking at the Knot

ACKNOWLEDGEMENTS

Thank you again to my dear friend and editor Karen Holmes who has encouraged and guided me throughout and to Catherine Cousins and the team at 2QT for all their help.

My gratitutude to Kevin Jackson of Beacon Computers for his patience in helping me understand the misunderstandings I have with computers.

To the Lakeland Dialect Society for their help with the spelling of half forgotten words.

Most of all thank you to the friends and neighbours within the small community in which I am priviledged to live for their support and many kindnessess.

Yesterday upon the stair I met a man who wasn't there, he wasn't there again today, I do so wish he'd go away.

William Hughes Mearns 1875–1965

For years we fooled ourselves. Now we can tell that how everyone our age heads for the brink.

Clive James 1939–2019

CHAPTER 1

On that day, the day he turned sixteen, the two most important people in Connor's life were his best friend Seb – his only friend, if push came to shove – and Miss, who tried to teach him. The person to whom he had been really close, his only *true* friend, his great-grandma Nan, had died three years previously. That was in the wrong order, for she had outlived her son.

According to Nan, Connor's granddad had moved south when jobs in the north were scarce, and he had died in his fifties. Connor's grandma had gone off with some fellow when Dad was still a boy and he had been sent north to be looked after by Nan. There he had met Mum, and Connor had been the result.

Connor wished his dad could have met someone different and that he could have had a mother who understood him, but he also understood that he couldn't put the clock back and you have to accept who you are and make the best of it.

In a way Nan's death had been a physical release, for the house was not built to home three generations. Originally it was two-up two-down, with a scullery and an outside privy until Dad had built the extension to make it three-up, three-down. He'd put in a proper kitchen with a downstairs toilet tacked on at the end, which meant you had to go through the kitchen if you were caught short. Connor had noted that very old people got caught short more often than most. Perhaps it had been a good thing that his grandparents had moved south.

A wheelchair and two Zimmer frames dominated the narrow hallway, and there was no room for bikes and skateboards. The odour of urine was dried into the carpet, its stains invisible amongst the orange chrysanthemums patterned into the earth-brown Axminster. The dark wallpaper made the space feel narrow and confined.

Connor never resented any of this. He loved having old Nan live with them for she had stories to tell of a different age when people were allowed to speak out, before the new age of witches with their covens of snowflakes and wokedom. Nan still believed in Jesus and read out things from the Bible, and she made them sound interesting and not preachy. She told him parables and said things like, 'It is easier for a camel to pass through the eye of a needle than it is for a rich man to enter the Kingdom of God.' She had tried to explain its meaning, but in the end he'd had to find the courage to put up his hand in class and brave the sniggers of his peers and the whispered comment, 'Con's got the hots for Miss.'

'What does this mean, Miss?' He read the quote, which he had carefully written down with Nan's help.

'It's a metaphor, Connor.' The bell rang before he had time to ask what a metaphor was, and the lesson was forgotten.

Nan had also said that 'the meek will inherit the earth', but Connor knew that no way would that ever happen. He also knew that no way would he do or say anything that might weaken or question Nan's faith, so he kept quiet and remembered the stories she had to tell.

And what stories they were; she used to read to him in the evening and fill his thoughts with such stuff as dreams and memories are made of – *Little Black Sambo, The Secret Garden, Alice in Wonderland and Through the Looking Glass, The Moon and Sixpence, Strewwelpeter,* bible stories and their numerous quotes.

He remembered another of her quotes: 'You cannot worship God and Mammon', but at that time he hadn't known what Mammon was.

In the last, bedridden year of her life, Nan would sing Irish folk songs to him in her fading, lilting brogue, her weary weak lungs rasping with bronchitis but her eyes a-twinkle with the nonsense words: *'There was a frog lived in a well, whip see-diddledee-dan deedee, harem scarem- diddle um dare-um, whip see-diddledee – dan deedee'.* Their hands were entwined as they tapped out the rhythm on the eiderdown.

Those words stayed with him, leaving little space in his young mind for the enforced retention of mathematics. He had coped well with simple sums, but when he went to big school the quagmire of geometry and algebra lay in wait. After that, if you made the grade, there were other incomprehensible things for which the nerds were given prizes and eventually whisked off to university. Connor's brain wanted no part of it.

There were no books in Nan's home when she was his age. Her parents had left the poverty of Eire to seek a new life in Glasgow, and she'd been placed in service at the age of fifteen with a middle-class family with three children and aspirations of becoming lower-upper.

'Live in, all found, 8/6d a week, uniforms provided'; the terms of employment were vague. Nan was a sort of house and parlour maid, and she also looked after the children. That meant that at half-past three in the afternoon, she had to change her clothes from a striped cotton frock, plain white pinny and silly white cap into a plain maroon frock with lacy sleeves and frilly white apron. Her matching headdress was kept in place by a black velvet bow.

A cook was employed to deal with the meals and keep the kitchen clean. Cook didn't live in but within brisk walking distance across the park, in a long, drab terrace of back-to-back houses. But her street had a strong community spirit. Ragged children with happy eyes played outside, kicking a tin barefoot along the wet cobbles, suspicious of the clean-booted children with their wooden hoops and skipping ropes beyond the park trees.

After the poverty of Ireland, this was high living and it was where Nan had been introduced to books. She had learnt the basics of reading at the village school in County Wicklow, *CAT* and *MAT* written on a slate with a piece of chalk, and the children in her new home were keen to further her education. They were given books on their birthdays, which they shared with her.

Nan's birthday was easy to remember; she went with the years. Connor looked forward to Nan's birthday more than his own and made her little presents out of plywood using his fretsaw to carve out a heart or a crucifix and colouring it with any old crayons he could find. What he most enjoyed was the delight on her face, and the way she hugged him to her crotch when he was very little, the musty smell of her like the dust cover of an old book.

Once he had given his mother a home-made present on her birthday, but she hadn't recognised it as such and used it as kindling to light the fire.

Connor hadn't got on with his real mother, but he'd learnt to put up with her maternal nagging. From an early age he recognised her disappointment as she rolled her eyes up to Heaven as if somehow that might solve the situation. Connor knew he was responsible for her dreams being shattered; unlike Nan, his mother didn't believe in Heaven, she believed in the eleven plus. She expected him to be the first in the family to go to grammar school, something to boast about to the neighbours, but Connor knew he was never going to get his eleven-plus. He had never been good at ticking the correct boxes.

When he had tried to master maths, poring over his homework and the complexities of long division alone in his bedroom without any help from his parents, the raised voices and anger infiltrated the room. They seemed to be absorbed in the *Star Wars* wallpaper and appeared to come out of the mouth of the giant poster of David Bowie on the wall. Even with his hands over his ears, Connor could still hear the shouting.

It was the haste of those domestic turnarounds that created the friction. Like some ghastly relay race to be run and won, Mum would return home late at 6.20am, exhausted from her night shift in the care home where she cleaned up the incontinence of strangers, and hand the baton to Dad. Her lateness made him late clocking in at the building site, and that provoked rancour, resentment and recriminations expressed in raised voices. That was the only way they knew how to express themselves.

Much as Connor would have preferred not to be an only child and had secretly wished for a younger sibling to help him bear the brunt of his mother, had there been one his bedroom would no longer have been his own. It was his private world, and all he had to do to keep in touch with those on the outside was to stroke the latest bit of technology Mum had given him to keep him quiet, and which Miss had described as digital crack cocaine. If he felt hungry and Mum had forgotten to put something out for him, he could nip to Burger King around the corner and get some chips for himself and Nan.

He didn't blame his parents; they did their best under difficult circumstances and he admired them for not putting Nan in a home when it was obvious that her presence put a strain on their relationship. Nan was Dad's grandma, not Mum's, and his upbringing was deep-rooted in his Irish Catholic childhood when generations stayed together and all was Hail Marys and guilt.

And then something happened, almost a year to the day after Connor had failed his eleven plus. His mother left and Gloria arrived.

It had all happened behind closed doors, as though someone had switched channels on the telly. Suddenly the nagging ceased and there was Gloria, all lovely brash blonde and smiley. She smelt delicious, was overweight and felt like a marshmallow when she hugged him. He hugged her back, even though he suspected he shouldn't now he was thirteen and beginning to have curious sensations.

Gloria didn't go out to work and spent most of the time painting her nails and watching cooking programmes, but she didn't just watch the programmes, she put the culinary lessons into practice. She sent Connor to the supermarket to buy all sorts of ingredients he had never heard of, like avocados and aubergines and olive oil.

Connor's dad started whistling again.

***

Miss had warned Connor that Seb was a bad influence but, as he was the only friend on offer, Connor had ignored her advice. Anyway, he probably knew Seb better than Miss did – though he could see what she was getting at. Seb took the mickey in class and drew attention to himself, putting out his tongue and taking selfies of it, passing his phone around the class whilst Miss was trying to maintain some kind of control.

Connor knew that Miss was struggling just as much as he was. Straight out of university, she was obviously out of her depth as she endeavoured to instil Shakespeare into unreceptive minds on the back row. Ofsted's report had painted the school in glowing colours, praising its integrated community and awarding accolades for its multiculturalism. Connor had doubts about this; he felt sorry for Miss and the other staff who had to teach Shakespeare in seventeen different languages. Was this what Nan had meant when she talked about speaking in tongues?

Miss raised her voice, almost shouted, 'Shakespeare was one of your antecedents.'

'An anti what, Miss?' Seb again trying to be clever.

Miss ignored him and tried another tack. 'Did you know that when you say things like "vanishing into thin air" and "you're not going to budge an inch", you are quoting Shakespeare?'

She still hadn't caught their attention so she decided to make it more personal. 'If you bid me good riddance and want to send me packing, if you think I am an eyesore, a laughing stock, the devil incarnate and you wish I was as dead as a doornail, you are quoting Shakespeare.'

Seb, who was busy mentally undressing Miss, called out, 'You're certainly not an eyesore, Miss.'

The bell rang and Connor saw the relief in Miss's eyes. He wanted to go up and give her a hug, like the ones Nan had given him when his real mum had shouted at him and Nan could see the tears welling up.

He understood why Miss had nearly shouted and he understood why his real mum had shouted, but his mum had done it in a malicious way, a personal way, blaming him and

Dad for her own unhappiness.

Dad shouted more than anyone, swearing like a trooper, but his shouting was not personal so it didn't hurt; his shouting was at the world in general and generally aimed at those to whom he was beholden for his livelihood. 'Bloody foreign oligarchs, ripping up the foundations and cellars of that beautiful old house to build an underground cinema.'

Connor had asked Dad once about Great-Grandad because Nan had told him little; it was as though she didn't want to talk about her husband.

'Your great-grandad understood underground,' Dad had said. 'He was apprenticed as a welder in Glasgow's shipyards. Unemployment drove him south to seek his fortune in London's sewers. He came to love the work, trained as a stonemason and admired those who had created those vast networks. Every handmade brick and shaped stone was placed not only for its utility but to please the eye. The tunnels led to vaulted areas like miniature underground cathedrals, where a man could stand up straight. The rats became the men's communicants. They learnt to trust them, took the crumbs from their bait boxes, learnt the time of day when Eucharist was held as man's excrement flowed freely by.'

Now there was sadness in his voice. 'It's all changed now. People tell me the sewers no longer run freely and the rats no longer go to communion. They are satiated, fattened by profligacy, baby wipes, nappies and congealed fat.'

Connor was unsure what profligacy was, and he knew his dad was about to kick off again. 'Why the bloody hell do we have to tolerate these rich bloody southerners coming north, buying up everything?' Dad demanded.

***

Having never passed an exam in his life, Connor's dad had a sneaking admiration for his son's failures, for he knew that Connor had inherited his own feral wisdom. If the end of the world was fast approaching, as the Extinction Rebellion expounders prophesied, it would be common sense and brawn which would survive when the world was choking for breath, not the possession of a Master's in English literature.

Connor's first breath had not been without controversy. There had been mutterings about teenage disasters, accidents happening, the word 'illegitimate' banded about. Connor's carrot-coloured hair had caused comment. There were sly glances, and relatives gossiped. He must be a throwback; Auntie Maureen, who felt she was a cut above her relatives and who was doing a course in genetics at the Open University, said, 'Recessive gene,' in a knowing sort of way.

With the weight of the Catholic church and Nan's strong beliefs, Connor's mum and dad had been pressured into marriage when they were too young. Dad had told his son all this when Connor was five and standing behind him doing what Dad called 'man's work', holding a screwdriver and passing it over when instructed.

This story about his hair had created an early uncertainty in Connor about who he actually was, and he thought about it constantly. He had mentioned it to Nan before she died. 'Absolute rubbish. That's your mother's side of the family stirring up trouble as usual,' she had replied.

Now, when he couldn't sleep having overstimulated his brain playing video games until midnight, he sank beneath the duvet and again felt Nan's warm presence and remembered the tales she'd told about her old man, Connor's great-grandfather, talking as if he were there alive, reminding herself of someone she'd loved, remembering he was still with her.

'How he loved his work and his family. He was a stonemason, loved the feel of the hardness of stone and the softness of my body, he did. He did a bit of drystone walling. He could look at a pile of stone and see where each one would fit. He never put a stone down to try another one, never picked a stone up twice. He was like that with me. Always considerate, always took off his outside boots at the door.'

Connor's freckles came later.

***

Now he had left school he would miss Miss. She had said encouraging things like, 'You have real promise, Connor,' which made him feel good. That had initiated comments from Seb, 'Oh, Miss has got the hots for Connor,' and a good deal of smirking from the back row.

The first three rows in the overcrowded classroom had been grabbed by the Asian pupils. They came from cultured backgrounds where discipline was not a dirty word. Some of them spoke three languages, whereas Connor's compatriots could hardly master their own.

Connor had plucked up courage to ask Miss a question. During citizenship classes he heard her use the word 'profligate' and wanted to know what it meant. It was something to do with waste and he needed to know; something had sparked it off in his memory, something Dad had said about the sewers of London and how the rats were no longer friendly. 'Pro what, Miss?'

But Seb had got in first. 'My mum had one of those. She had a ring inside her to keep it up and Dad said it put her off sex.' Sniggering took over and Miss was out of her depth again. Connor's question went unanswered.

***

Little did Connor know at that time that he was about to come face to face with a cornucopia of profligacy. The Holy Grail of profligacy was about to be within his grasp – although he didn't know exactly what the Holy Grail was. There had been something about it on the telly that had caught his attention. It was something which everyone in the world was looking for but, just as he'd settled down with a cushion to watch it on the big telly in the kitchen, his dad had come in, grabbed the zapper from him and switched to *Strictly Come Dancing*.

***

Connor was pleased he'd got the job, though it was not what he had hoped for. Having already decided that school had taught him nothing of real value, he'd jumped at the chance to say goodbye to it. His chances of winning *Britain's Got Talent* were remote, so the promise of a yellow fluorescent jacket would give him an aura of authority, which he did not feel but felt he deserved.

On his first day he wanted to be early, create a good impression, so he gave himself plenty of time to cycle the eight miles to the recycling plant. As he turned into the impressive high-wired, security-gated complex, a voice called, 'Wheresta think thous ga'an wid that?'

Connor dropped his bike on a small grassy bank.

'Shouldn't leave it there, sonny – they'll pick it up and it'll be through t'crusher before you can say how's your uncle.'

From a pillbox cabin on the right of the concrete drive, above which was a sign saying CHECK IN, emerged a larger-than-life figure, his Benidorm tan and steroid-fed muscles fighting for recognition and space in a covering of dark-blue tattoos. His hard hat was white and too small and had been put on at a jaunty angle which, if push came to shove, Connor thought was incapable of protecting him from anything. On the man's top half was nothing other than the coveted yellow fluorescent jacket. His large belly button was showing and his tight jeans barely covered his backside. Connor giggled to himself, thinking, *I could post a letter between his buttocks.*

'Wasta laffing at sonny?' The man came forward, his hand outstretched in an act of friendship. 'Call me Dave,' he said.

Connor did not know then, but would quickly discover, that however repellent Dave's exterior inside him was a sangfroid, a decency and good humour. But at that stage Connor had no concept of sangfroid, had never heard the word; he did not realise that this meeting would be the start of his real education.

He dutifully placed his bike outside the gates, hoping it would not get pinched, and followed Dave into the cabin to be issued with his own yellow jacket. On the back was printed CONNOR. For the first time in his life, he knew who he was.

Dave said, 'Follow me,' and stepped into the vast concrete complex, a labyrinth of bunkers as far as the eye could see. They were piled high, each section clearly marked. The concrete driveway was spotless. Connor started to admire Dave; here was a man on top of his job like his own dad, unlike Miss who wasn't.

Although the compartments were labelled, Dave felt it necessary to explain each one. He thought that Connor, who had not managed to pass GCSE English or maths, was incapable of reading and he was trying to be helpful. They passed textiles, glass, paper, cans and foil, plastics, asbestos, TVs and monitors, fridges and freezers, large appliances, car batteries and oil. Up a slight incline, around the corner, they met up with plasterboard and gypsum, tyres, garden waste and scrap metal. Dave read out each one. He stopped at small appliances and commented, 'That's where people toss their old laptops and computers. They don't always remember to remove the hard drives, especially when they're in a hurry.'

There were containers for mixed wood, cardboard, non-recyclable waste, hard plastic (toys, buckets, bowls, plastic furniture), rubble and soil and, above this section in large letters, a stern message NO PLASTERBOARD, NO GYPSUM, NO ASBESTOS HERE PLEASE, for those who had missed the correct slot and couldn't be bothered to retrace their steps. They would have to go round again like musical chairs, no U-turns allowed.

Connor was impressed but kept his thoughts to himself. He thought instead about Miss, remembering vividly that day when he had tried to ask his question and Miss had written 'prof' on the blackboard. When the catcalls started, led by Seb, Connor thought what his fellow pupils needed was a good cuff behind the ear. He was certain that Dave, had he been there, would have given them one.

CHAPTER 2

He had been there for three months when they came. Connor noticed them for they were different, not the usual Sunday-morning couple ditching their rubbish before nipping round the corner for a pub lunch. They were in a white Enterprise hired van.

He saw her first. She was beautiful, tall and willowy like a model, but more genuine. She was not dark but milk-chocolate brown, a slight hump of pregnancy beneath her flowing thin cotton garment, its bright colours reflected in the vehicle's window. She wore bangles which clinked as she stretched out her arm to help a child out of the van.

Connor, who was just thinking about his lunch break, acted on Dave's advice about always being considerate towards people and called out, 'Can I help you?'

As he approached the van a man emerged from the driver's door, tall and bronzed, his tan of long standing, not like Dave's which had come from ten days on the Costa Brava. His face was furrowed and his hair a mass of conker-coloured curls. 'Thank you, that would be good of you. We're in a bit of a hurry – we have a plane to catch in Manchester in three hours' time. We've been cleaning out some things from my grandmother's home. It should have been done years ago. She lived in the same house for sixty years, so this is just the start. We'll have to come back again later in the year.'

The little boy was now out of the van, helping with the less heavy items, Connor put him at about five or six years old. 'Are you going on holiday?' he asked.

'Unfortunately not. We're going back to Syria with my NGO.'

Connor would like to have asked what an NGO was, but the man was struggling to lift a heavy computer out of the back of the van. 'Where should I put this?'

'Just round the corner. There's a sign.'

The man climbed into the van again and drove the few extra yards as Connor, the child and the woman followed on foot. She said, 'You have an interesting job. Do you enjoy your work?'

His answer went unheard, for the man had thrown the computer into its correct place, and it hit the concrete with a thud. Then the family were gone with a cheery, 'Nice to meet you.'

Connor decided he would take a look the next day to see if the hard drive was still in there. He would need a screwdriver to prise off the front; he was about to ask Dave if he had one but thought better of it. Dave had said something about it being 'agin the rules'.

He would take one from Dad's toolbox and return it before Dad had a chance to miss it, for Dad didn't lend things. Dad called his toolbox sacrosanct and no one was allowed to touch it. 'Neither a borrower nor a lender be,' he would say.

Later, as he hid the screwdriver down his jeans, Connor remembered that was another of his Nan's sayings, along with God and Mammon. He felt guilty on two fronts. It struck him that the borrowing-lending thing had a point; the wealthy lent and got richer, and the poor borrowed and got poorer. That was probably why Seb's mum, who was on benefits, was always going on about loan sharks when she wasn't in the bookies.

Connor couldn't sleep that night as he tried to think of a way to smuggle the computer beyond the confines of the complex. It was too big and cumbersome to carry home on his bicycle, you couldn't just slip it into your jeans like a smartphone – but you could slip in a screwdriver.

When he finally levered the front off the computer, his guilt abated. He had an overwhelming feeling of elation; perhaps he was about to find his Holy Grail. His immediate problem was identifying the hard drive amongst all the parts; how would he be able to access its contents after it was detached from its provider? He wished now that he'd gone to those after-school computer classes.

He must try and keep calm in case someone came and he had to pretend he was doing a bit of sorting. He started to whistle like his dad did when faced with uncertainty and pleasant anticipation.

Thinking that the hard drive might be near the power button, he tugged at the first moveable-looking part. It came away. As it lay impotent, waiting to find a new host, he never imagined for one moment that he held the rest of his life in his hands.

Connor remembered Seb talking about a thing called a caddy, which could connect two incompatible machines. Then another thought struck him: what if the data could only be accessed with a password? Of course, Seb would know what to do but he couldn't be trusted with a secret.

His step-mum Gloria might know. Connor trusted her; her outside image, rather like Dave's, sent out the wrong message. Gloria didn't look like a geek but Nan used to say that you couldn't judge a book by its cover. Had Nan still been alive, she might have described Gloria as 'a bit of a floozy', but not in a nasty way – more in an understanding, affectionate way.

When Dad wasn't there, Connor would try to bring computers into the conversation in a couldn't-care-less way while he and Gloria watched *Who Wants to be a Millionaire?* together.

That night, during the ads, he asked, 'Gloria, do you know anything about computers?'

'Not a lot, pet. What do you want to know?'

Even at sixteen, he loved being called pet by Gloria. 'Can you transfer a hard drive into another computer?'

'Well, the hard drive will need to be used with the same operating system. Why do you want to know?'

Connor knew he would have to tell a white lie. 'It's just something I saw on the telly.' He hated lying to someone he trusted, but Gloria had become curious.

'Tell you what,' she said. 'My sister has a Polish boyfriend and he goes round skips collecting out-of-date electrical stuff. He's a dab hand at making a living out of nothing. He runs the whole thing by word of mouth from their bedroom – it's piled high with bits of wire and things. I don't think he should really be in this country, but what the hell. He doesn't bother anyone and he makes my sister happy, which is a job in itself. Next time I see him, I'll ask him.' She turned up the sound on the TV.

For a week, the hard drive burnt a hole in Connor's pocket. He wanted to ask Gloria if she'd had a chat with the Polish guy but did not wish to appear too keen. It was a week later, as he wandered into the kitchen looking for something to eat, that Gloria said, 'Oh, by the way, I had a word with Vitold. Kim helped him write this down. I can't make head nor tail of it.'

Taking the grubby piece of paper from her hand, Connor looked at the pencilled notes and thanked her. Forgetting that he was hungry, he went upstairs to his room and read: *Hard drive needs to be plugged into computer with same operating system using a sata cable. Click on storage device icon to select – permission to access dialogue box appears. Right click to access drop down menu – select properties, select security, select advanced, select change ownership.*

If he could find a compatible computer, Connor felt he could manage the instructions. He kicked himself for not having noted the make of the thrown-away computer, but it was too late now. He had imagined that somehow he could just plug the thing into any old machine.

He would have to go and see this Polish guy and make some excuse. He went downstairs again. Gloria was still in the kitchen. 'Gloria, this guy shacked up with your sister, he sounds interesting. I'd like to meet him.'

'Okay, next time I go over you can come with me.'

It was another ten days before she said, 'I'm going to pop over and see Kim this evening. Do you want to come with me? It'll give you a chance to meet her and her Polish bloke.'

***

The house was on the other side of town in a run-down area. After the initial introductions and beer and crisps, Vitold and Connor went up to the bedroom. It was packed to the ceiling with old boxes of technical stuff, wires everywhere – you could hardly see the bed. Into Connor's head came a picture of his newly acquired step-auntie Kim and this Polish guy on the mattress, getting up to Heaven knows what.

Connor produced the hard drive from his pocket and said, 'Don't suppose you have a computer compatible with this, and a sata cable?'

Vitold looked at it. 'Somewhere. Somewhere I find.'

18

Just as Connor had taken a shine to Dave, he immediately took a shine to Vitold. He sensed that under their skins, but differently wrapped, were the same decent people. Dave was overweight, no bones visible, red skinned in the few spaces free of tattoos, and clean shaven to the top of his head. Vitold was thin, pale with visible veins, his protruding cheekbones almost hidden by heavy stubble and topped by greying, receding hair. It was clear to Connor that Vitold was much cleverer than Dave but less efficient.

Suddenly, with a grunt of satisfaction, Vitold swooped down to a large box near the door and fished out a computer. Connor looked at it; there, as clear as daylight, were the scuffs on the casing he'd made with his dad's screwdriver. It was too much of a coincidence – someone was on his side. Someone had faith

Connor said, 'Is it for sale?' and proffered a five-pound note

'No money. No money. I like your auntie. Why you want? I carry for you.'

Connor didn't reply.

It took him two weeks to get it up and running.

***

Connor switched on the computer and read: *Surrounded by the beauty of nature, it is an arrogance, an indulgence of human-kind not to believe in God. To think we are omnipotent, beyond reproach, living in our solipsistic bubble, unable to accept that there is a greater power out there. I shall have to cross swords with Kafka.*

Blimey, thought Connor, I hope it's not all like this. Who the bloody hell was Kafka? Wasn't there a band called Kafka? Maybe this person had known him – or them – and Connor had hit the jackpot. He Googled Kafka on his Smartphone and was none the wiser. There was a fashion house with that name in Aberdeen, and something called Apache Kafka, an open-source stream-processing platform, and some German guy. None of them were any use to him at that moment.

He continued reading. *How easily I turned my back on the reassuring messages of hope, faith and trust taught me when a child. Had I not been watching* Flog It *on that wet afternoon, it would still be buried in my subconscious.*

Connor remembered his nan used to be glued to programmes about antiques, though she had never owned anything of any value.

There it was on the screen, the ornate gilded frame encasing a painting of a boyish Jesus with blond hair, his arms outstretched, welcoming the world within a triptych, emerging from a darkened forest, surrounded by animals, with three children sitting at his feet listening. On either side close to the frame stood an angel, wings folded, holding bowls of fruit and flowers. The header was 'All things bright and beautiful' and the footer was 'The Lord God made them all'. The expert said it was a Margaret Tarrant.

This was not a man talking, Connor thought. It was more like Miss, more like his nan. He had somehow assumed it would be a man and he felt a little disappointed.

He was about to continue reading when he remembered where he had seen that painting before. He recognised the description; Nan had a small copy of it, more like a postcard, in her special memory box. After Nan died, it had been thrown out by his real mother who was keen to get rid of the last vestige of her unloved grandmother-in-law.

So, this could not be a coincidence. It was fate; he'd been destined to find this hard drive. God had somehow made Connor fail his GCSEs, otherwise he would not have been working at the recycling plant, would not have found the hard drive.

He wondered who this woman was. She must be pretty ancient because those people who'd thrown away the computer had looked to be in their late thirties, and she'd been their grandmother. The woman had looked older than the man, but it was more difficult to tell with coloured people.

Connor's mind raced as he continued to read.

Am seeing things clearly now, not through a glass darkly. It hung on the wall at the end of my bed, a permanent fixture from the age of three. I saw it as I awoke and as my eyes closed before sleep for all those years, until my beloved home, my sanctuary, was sold to others, my childhood possessions dispersed and I was out in the big wide world. I was made to put away childish things too soon.

These were definitely the ramblings of some old biddy. Connor had no idea what he might find, or how much of it there was. Nothing was dated so he couldn't tell when the ramblings had started or when they might finish. Having got this far and made all that effort, however, he decided he'd keep going. He'd read a little each day; there might be something more interesting later on, something he could relate to.

The Father, the Son and the Holy Spirit are buried deep; my Trinity has become Bob Dylan, my computer and a litre bottle of Famous Grouse. I have even started flirting with Islam and can understand where all these extremists are coming from.

Blimey, thought Connor, was she a terrorist? He thought about informing the police; it might be rather fun and he'd probably get a mention on TV and become a hero. Then he remembered he'd get into trouble for stealing the hard drive. Anyway, if the old biddy was already dead what was the point of reporting her?

CHAPTER 3

I never imagined the end of my life could be so full of uncertainty. Having reached my years of discretion, I have had plenty of time to get things right but I have wasted it. My time has been consumed by trying to get things right in the eyes of other people. Somewhere along the line, I took my eye off the ball, lost my ability to catch it; then the balls and the games changed.

I can still remember that reassuring soft thud of a grey, balding tennis ball hitting the sagging catgut of a tennis racket that had been left outside without its press. I can still remember the muffled laughter of parents drifting through the open window on a summer's evening when compulsory bedtime came too early and the sun was still high in the sky and it was too hot for sleep. I can still remember when there was reassurance – when Incy Wincy Spider was still able to climb up the spout again. Then I was so certain.

Of course, now my mind refuses to leave me alone. There are all those years of regret, and the guilt of not having kept a diary. 'Write things down, put down what you are thinking,' my mother used to say. When it was too late, when the years had passed and the pages remained blank, I assuaged my guilt by telling myself that my jottings would be of no value. Historians wouldn't waste their time pondering over schoolgirl crushes on my brothers' friends and trying to be grown up before your time. Neither would they want to know about my appointments with doctors, dentists, hairdressers, solicitors and the endless social events, all scribbled down in an unreadable hand. Unimportant squiggles.

Am certain that the last bad fall did something to my brain. I think it affected it in a most positive way, gave it a bloody good shake up.

Falling has become commonplace – my mind and body now fail to synchronise. My mind is much younger than my body and it is becoming resentful at having the responsibility of looking after its elderly attachment.

The fall itself was both traumatic and a bit of a hoot. It must have happened about midday, for when the first responder arrived at seven in the evening my lunch had turned to charcoal in the Aga. I found it the following morning. What awoke me, after presumably being unconscious for a few hours, was a cold breeze on the top of my head; I had fallen by the half-open back door and hit my head on the stone step. Unable to get up, I had to call for help. Fortunately Evie was taking her dog for its evening walk and she found me, but she couldn't lift me, despite my elderly diminished weight, and called the first responders.

Living in a small village, I know most of the first responders quite well. It was young Gordon who dragged me to my feet. In real life he is a bit of a tearaway. He was determined to call for an ambulance, so I had to be quite firm with him and told him that if he did I would never speak to him again.

He asked me to stand on one leg for half a minute, tell him what day it was, the names of my children and that of the Prime Minister, then to follow his finger with my eyes. After all that, he said I was alright. Asking the name of the Prime Minister was a mistake on Gordon's part because it apparently solicited a stream of abuse from me about politicians, of which I have no recollection.

Next morning, the lump on the back of my head was the size of a tennis ball and my mind went into overdrive. News of my fall circulated and with it the certainty that it was due to my long-standing close association with the holy spirit. Someone had been monitoring the bottles in my wheelie bin.

My faith has taken a bit of a knock recently. It is very difficult to find anyone with whom I can discuss things face to face, who may be interested in the struggles going on in my mind, the feud between the different parts of my brain. There are well-meaning discussion groups and social services, but my mind is pleading with me not to get caught up in their nets. They put labels on people and at my age I have no wish to be classified.

There are times when I have convinced myself that I am going barmy or doolally or whatever. I'm sure my family think so, and the village certainly does. 'Oh, to see ourselves as others see us' – who said that? Was it that Robbie Burns from over the border, who had a memorial in every port?

I have done some unforgiveable things in my life about which I feel more ashamed as I get older. I have done things that I ought not to have done but I keep them to myself for fear of exposure, of retribution. Not retribution from God, for I hope He sees only the good in me as I have tried to see only the good in others during the last decade of my life.

The media assails us with false prophets who give credence to dishonesty, transgression, immorality and selfishness as though they are the heights of sophistication and culture. There are new gods out there, and Christ is back in His Sepulchre.

To cheer myself up, am listening to Bob Dylan, 'Like a Rolling Stone'. Very appropriate, though he always makes me reach for the whisky bottle.

***

'Who *is* this old biddy?' Connor wondered. And as he was wondering, suddenly Miss came into his head and he felt an unexpected rush of love for her. She had tried her best to get him through school; now he was hearing her voice again. They were re-connecting and here, alone and outside the classroom, he was able to listen. Those quotes from Shakespeare and others were coming into focus; the dark glass of Seb was no longer there. Miss had warned him about dancing attendance on Seb – and hadn't Miss said that 'dancing attendance' came from Shakespeare?

He continued reading.

***

Today I almost threw in the towel and accepted the fact that my mind is digitally barren. I rang up *The Times* and the BBC twice in order to be heard, for though I can type onto a computer I have never mastered the art of choosing the correct button to press with confidence to send my thoughts flying to all corners of the globe. Probably a blessing. It is difficult to apologise at the best of times, and to say it on line must be nigh on impossible. Statistics tell me there are more than two or three million octogenarians living in the UK, the waste-not-want-not generation, unheard, left behind, disenfranchised because we are too old to learn a new language or new tricks, unable to share our experiences with the new generation. We're not given that last minute chance to contribute.

My hearing aid has packed up again. It is an NHS one and pretty efficient, but putting in a new battery is so fiddly. My stiff old fingers cannot hold the tiny batteries and I usually end up dropping the damned things. They disappear under the sideboard and I cannot get down on my hands and knees to find them. Actually, I can get down but I can't get up again.

You'd think that when scientists and engineers can send a man to the moon, their energies might have been better spent on designing an inexpensive utility device that the NHS could afford and would benefit the whole of mankind.

I am becoming a grumpy old woman. I must try and detach that part of me for it is not how I really feel. It is just that sometimes this other person gets the better of me.

But it won't get the better of me today. It is a glorious day, warm and sunny at 6.30am and not a cloud in the sky. I put out stuff to be recycled in my dressing gown; they always come early and if I miss them the four-week build-up of bottles becomes an embarrassment when it is left in the road.

I didn't go back to bed as usual with a cup of tea but dressed and sat on the old seat at the bottom of the garden under the oak tree next to the beech hedge. Though younger than me, the seat is showing its age, probably through neglect. One end is completely rotten and covered in moss and bird droppings. Recently I have felt drawn to it again because it is where Hugh and I used to sit so many decades ago, when the oak was still a sapling and the beech hedge a line of newly planted whips. That was when we could still talk with one another.

The oak tree grew from an acorn picked up at Boscobel. It is a descendant of the mighty oak that gave Charles II sanctuary when he was being hunted by the Roundheads. I remember Hugh pocketing half a dozen of the acorns and using them as a kind of history lesson for Sarah, our first-born child, who was three at the time. He gave her a little history lesson on one of those weekend family outings to a stately home. He whetted her appetite for stories, sowed the seeds of Sarah's interest in history. No surprise she eventually became a historian and academic.

The acorns spent their first years in pots. Born in Staffordshire, transported to Lancashire and Yorkshire as Hugh changed jobs and new roots were established, before finally arriving in Cumbria as saplings to be planted out. In the same way, I returned to my roots. Now half a century old, they are mature. I can see one of them as I lie in bed; the other day a pair of red squirrels were courting, running up and down the trunk in a frenzy of excitement.

The area in which it now lives has become a mini-woodland. Snowdrops and bluebells have taken over where once there was lawn and early risings of midges and flies. Their bites make sitting there without a covering of insect repellent a risky business

One end of the bench looks sound enough. It is firm to the touch and covered in the most beautiful silvery-sage, yellowing lichen, each piece of which is differently shaped like paper doily and is rough to the touch. I sat down and drank my tea, half-dozing again, pleased I'd dragged myself away from the comfort of my bed and my obsessive watching of the news with its constant messages of travail and mistrust.

Music was coming from next door – it sounded like Vivaldi, but that was just a guess. It had a soporific effect and I was dozing off again when I noticed the aroma. At first I thought it must be scent of the philodendron but it was too early. Then I heard the clink of glass and recognised the smell and, in my half-awake state, I was a child again.

I was back in the kitchen, standing on a chair, stirring the cauldron of simmering raspberries with a huge wooden spoon to prevent them sticking to the bottom, waiting until they were reduced sufficiently to add the sugar under Mother's watchful eye. Being wartime, sugar was like gold dust and rationing had almost put a stop to jam making; the weekly ration was hardly enough to sprinkle on one's helping of porridge. Mother had saved it up for weeks so that the raspberries would not go to waste, and it had been supplemented by the rations of the six evacuees. The fear that I might spill a grain still haunts me.

My next-door neighbour is making jam and my mother is back with me again. Were she still alive, she would be one hundred and twenty-eight. Why, oh why, am I only beginning to appreciate her now? I suppose that as a child I was closer to my father; he gave the hugs and she gave the discipline. Mother wasn't a hugger but the discipline paid off.

I am so glad she died when she did. The new world would have made her unhappy. She was so generous all her life that she left it with no possessions, having given them all away to good causes. When she died, she had thirty-eight charitable direct debits. She took the adage 'to give and not to count the cost' a little too literally. She must have thought better of it when it was too late for I found a scribble on the back of a bank statement which said: *Have tried to cancel the direct debits to third world countries, suspect the money is being syphoned off by some dictator. And what is the point of saving all those children? They will just become cannon fodder in some future war.*

I am beginning to see Mother in a different light. Yesterday I was tempted to send a cheque to Water Aid. An emotion-grabbing short film on television of a small girl walking across a desert to collect water had got to me. It was followed by the news of a ten-year-old girl committing suicide after being bullied on social media. I wondered which of those two children was the happier.

Went indoors again when the insects became vengeful. One had already bitten me and I sensed others were waiting in the queue, and the flycatcher (whose pantry I had usurped) was waiting patiently for me to go.

On my way inside, I spotted Evie in the back lane up early walking her dog Bo Bo. He is a mongrel, although I am no longer allowed to call him a mongrel; he has a new name and is apparently a new breed. When Evie told me, it sounded like cock-a-leekie. In the winter he is forced to wear a tartan jacket. I know he doesn't like it because he looks up at me with doleful eyes. Evie saw me, waved and called out, 'Pleased to see you're upright.'

***

Connor chuckled, stopped reading and sat down on the bed. Seb's mum had a dog like that –she had bought it on the internet but never took it for walks.

He liked this old lady, but at the same time he felt a bit sorry for her. He understood how she'd feel if she got things wrong; he wondered if her mother would have shouted at her if she had spilled some of the sugar as his real mother would have done at him.

He continued reading.

***

Of course I didn't spill any. I remember how Mother used the setting of the jam as an allegory. At ten years old I hadn't a clue what an allegory was, but I still remember her words. She had scooped the impurities off the top of the jam onto a saucer and left them for a few minutes on the outside sill of the open kitchen window. She muttered to no one in particular, 'Scum always rises to the top,' and I knew she was not talking about the jam.

When the impurities were set, she tilted the saucer. The greyish substance remained firm but from underneath slowly flowed a trickle of clear raspberry-red juice. 'There you are.

29

There is always good waiting to be released beneath a crust of badness.' Then she poured the tiny quantity back into the pan for its final boil.

The sun was almost as warm as midday and I wanted to sit there longer. It made me think of Harry, the heat in the refugee camps, the lack of water, malnutrition and flies. How is he coping? Is he still in Syria or has he been moved on? I haven't heard from him for ages – I must remember to give Anna a ring. She may have heard from him; the umbilical cord between mother and son is rarely severed.

***

Connor realised that he had actually met Harry. The thought that he may have been one of the last people in this country to see him, other than people at the airport, gave him a strange feeling of importance. The old lady's writing was coming alive.

He stayed awake late all week, reading into the night. Yesterday he had almost been late for work. Dave had said nothing but there had been a roll of the eyes. Connor knew he would have to ration his reading.

Gloria was calling from downstairs. 'Hope you're not doing anything you shouldn't up there. Time to turn the light off. Goodnight, pet.'

He would read one more page.

CHAPTER 4

I've had a long chat with Anna. She has just heard from Harry – what a relief. He has been transferred to a short-term medical mission at Hatay in Turkey.

I turned on the news whilst I was still in bed, hoping for something about Syria but Syria has gone off the radar. In its place were thirty minutes of Me Toos whingeing on, mini celebs and film stars with provocative plunging necklines.

I made myself get up because Anna said that Matt might come over with a cow to eat off the grass in the paddock. I am so fortunate to have Matt as a son-in-law. We are only fifteen years apart in age, so we often see things in the same way. He understands my needs and that is why, every spring for the past twelve years since Hugh died, he has brought me an elderly cow with her final calf to be my summer companions.

He chooses my friends with care. 'She's seventeen, and this will be her last calf. When it's weaned, she will be off to the knackers and turned into cat and dog food. I want her to enjoy her last summer with you.'

I shall have to break the news of the cow to my next-door neighbours. They are newishly arrived to live in the village from London, having seen the house on some programme called *Escape to the Country*. The bush telegraph tells me they are called Crispin and Amanda, so they may find it difficult to fit in amongst the Freds and Elsies. Also, there will be the usual resentment that their London money has excluded the children of the Freds and Elsies from being able to afford to live in the village.

I hope they will be understanding. Their kitchen wall is part of the dividing wall between their property and my paddock, with its lovely view up to the high fells. It is where cows love to stand and scratch their bottoms along the sandstone window sill.

I shall ask them in for a welcoming drink and explain things, try to get off on the right foot as Mother would say. Poor Mary, who lives on the fringe of the village in a cottage close to the old vicarage, is having a difficult time with newcomers. The obsolete vicarage has been bought as a retreat for LGBT or LSDB, or something like that, and they have objected to her sheep eating the grass in the graveyard, which sheep have been doing since medieval times. They do a better job than a lawn mower because they can nibble close to the gravestones and anyway, it is difficult now to find someone who will give up a summer evening to cut the grass.

Mary thinks they are objecting because they are all vegans and they resent the fact that others think differently. She told them, 'If you feel that way, you shouldn't have come to live amongst farmers whose forbears were brought up on brawn and potted meat. You can't survive working in the fields on a lettuce leaf.' She has got off on the wrong foot.

When I finally met their leader, I put my foot in it by laughingly repeating Mary's words. 'When in Rome do as the Romans do. You're surrounded by farmers whose forbears were brought up on brawn and potted meat. They wouldn't have survived on a lettuce leaf.'

The leader didn't reply but I saw in her eyes that she had

labelled me as another untouchable. Or was it a he?

The struggle of dressing and undressing myself is exhausting and I could happily stay in bed for the whole day, but if I did that would be the end. 'She has taken to her bed,' the village would say.

***

Just like old Nan, Connor thought. He was starting to feel a responsibility for this old girl. Should he tell Gloria about her? But he sensed that the old biddy enjoyed her privacy and would be averse to exposure.

***

I wish had been sufficiently disciplined to keep a day-by-day diary instead of relying on my memory. For one of my birthdays, my parents gave me a five-year one, bound in red leather with a tiny golden lock and key. I can still feel its presence in my hand. I thought it such a beautiful thing, and I had no wish to defile it with my thoughts. But if I had, at least my thoughts would be in chronological order instead of scattered over nine decades and wrongly filed on my computer. They have been encouraged by Famous Grouse and become entangled with trans blues and Bob Dylan telling me not to worry, not to think twice about it.

It may be the last time I stand in line at the check-out in Morrison's, looking guiltily at the plastic-wrapped turnip in my trolley. Why on earth do they think it necessary to wrap a turnip in plastic? It has a skin like a rhino and one needs a hacksaw to peel it. Usually I find a turnip in the road that has fallen off a farmer's trailer, dislodged as he went round the corner too fast on his way to fodder his sheep.

The traffic goes too fast on the A66 – 'Get your kicks on

the A66, Gran,' my grandchildren say. During lockdown, Morrison's started delivering to old people living in remote areas. What a godsend. I never go near a doctor and I am not considered vulnerable, so getting a slot with other supermarkets was impossible unless you were prepared to spend a whole day on the phone.

My generation has never felt vulnerable. We are immune to physical hurt and attacks of emotional introspection and self-pity; as Hugh used to say, 'We didn't take out our entrails and examine them every five minutes. We just got on with life and learnt to value the right people.' And thus we make new friends along the way, like Stella who now delivers on Fridays.

When she hadn't arrived by 6pm last Friday, I started to worry about her because she would be on the A66. The phone rang at 6.30 and her reassuring voice said, 'Hello, Julia. Don't worry, the van broke down and we're waiting for a replacement. I'll be with you shortly.'

I said, 'Please don't worry. You've had a long day, leave it until tomorrow. My delivery isn't important.'

Stella arrived in a thunderstorm and got soaked to the skin as she ran across the yard. Conscious of her customer training, she addressed me from behind her mask as Mrs Lancaster, aware that she must respect the customer.

I said again, 'You've had a long day.'

'Yes, I started at seven this morning.'

Normally I would have given her a hug, but lockdown had made me wary.

***

Connor couldn't believe his luck – he now had a name for his old biddy. It gave him a sense of well-being ; although he was only calling her an old biddy in his mind, he sensed he was being disrespectful to someone of whom he was becoming fond.

***

The following evening, thanks to Stella delivering the wine and the fact that it was warm and we were allowed to sit outside, I invited Crispin and Amanda to pop over for a drink. They obviously wanted to make a good impression and were slightly overdressed; other than stud earrings, jewellery before six is a no-no in the real countryside. Old jeans and a body warmer will carry you through the whole day. Crispin had on a very smart blazer with embossed brass buttons and a cravat tucked into a pristine white shirt. I thought I'd better warn him about the cow, because cows are inclined to shit without warning.

They were smiley. Crispin held out his hand in greeting but remembered lockdown and withdrew it before it reached me, rather like coitus interruptus. They settled themselves down on the fold-up chairs I had managed to drag downstairs from the boxroom. Normally we would have sat around the kitchen table, but distancing is now the new norm and we must stay outside.

Hugh used to call the kitchen 'Sid's Café'. In the old days, I produced food for the contractors during silaging and shearing. It was a sensible ploy because a free meal ensured you got priority when the weather was fine and workers were in demand by every livestock farmer in the county.

I took quite a shine to Crispin and Amanda; they seem genuine people and will quickly adapt to Wellies. They are planning to keep hens. I didn't wish to appear a rural know-all but suggested six point-of-lay Maran pullets. I kept them as a child. They are rather beautiful, speckly dark-grey and white, which accentuates their red combs. They lay the loveliest dark brown eggs, each hen producing an individual depth of colour, shell texture and configuration of speckles. If you took note of which one was clucking madly and found a warm egg, you could match the hen and the egg.

My hens all had names. I remember one was called Henrietta and another we christened Floppy because of her floppy comb. She used to lay her eggs prematurely before the shell was properly formed. Being wartime and with food scarce, Mother would take a spoon and scoop the white and yolk into a cup for breakfast. However much grit we put in their feed to strengthen the shells, it made no difference.

I could tell Amanda wasn't really listening; that was probably just as well, for I sensed she may be hot on health and safety. But I did feel that I should warn them about the foxes if they were dead set on keeping hens. 'We are plagued by foxes so I would advise...'

Amanda interrupted in a paroxysm of delight. 'Oh, how wonderful! We love wildlife – we never miss Chris Packham and *Springwatch*. Isn't he wonderful? We feed the foxes. They come into our garden.'

I was about to destroy their celluloid illusions of the countryside, so I was cautious in my reply. 'Well, country foxes are not used to eating the leftovers from MacDonald's. They prefer fresh food, so I suggest your first purchase should be a sturdy hen house so that you can shut them in at night.'

My advice fell on deaf ears. Within six hours of the young pullets arrival, old Reynard had latched on to them and slaughtered the lot. There was a knock on my door and there was Amanda, tears streaming down her face, saying she wished they had stayed in London.

I was tempted to say 'I told you so' but didn't. I asked her in for a cup of coffee, although we were still in that no-man's area of semi-lockdown. To cheer her up, I suggested she might like to own a nannie goat with a kid. I said I would be happy for it to live in the paddock with the cow, and she could watch its progress from her kitchen window. She said she would think about it.

I must try and stop worrying about other people. It confuses my mind, and if I give a glint of a hint that I may be going gaga someone with a degree in psychology or medicine will join forces with social services and claim authority over me. They'll have me assessed and, unable to accept that going gaga is just part of growing old, my children will be bombarded with pamphlets from the NHS on how to deal with dementia.

I am convinced that growing old as a woman is less easy than growing old as a man. You become hidden from view. If you are male, your wrinkles become rugged and interesting; life is written into your face. Female wrinkles are not usually allowed on TV, though you do see clusters of female oldies on the telly, singing their hearts out on *Songs of Praise*.

I have always felt that prayer is too precious to allow itself to become a form of entertainment. Of course, I may be wrong – I probably am, for there is that quote in the New Testament: 'When two or three are gathered together in my name I shall grant their request'. I imagine that those good ladies are giving it a go, just like a night at the bingo.

The physical act of Holy Communion has become a struggle. Just getting to the altar rail is a challenge because I must find things to hold on to. Once I leave the certainty of the pews, there is that acreage to be crossed between the lectern and the pulpit before I can grab the end of the choir stalls. If I make it to the altar rail, getting up after kneeling is impossible without the help of half the congregation, which scuppers the sanctity of the moment.

Religion is a difficult thing to hold on to. The goodness and reassurance of faith is easier, and best found around the kitchen table. A whisky and a packet of crisps have replaced the sacrament.

Bob Dylan is singing something about feeling his love and I am sitting in front of my computer. The bright light of the computer screen has made my glaucoma play up, and the special glasses I need to deal with this situation have somehow found their way into kitchen.

After I went downstairs, instead of looking for my specs, I hung my stick on the edge of the sink and looked out of the kitchen window at the sky. The clouds were particularly beautiful, cumulus with flat bottoms and fluffy tops heralding fine weather.

I had a sudden urge to say the Lord's Prayer, which I did out loud. That I was word perfect after so many years amazed me and I repeated it, looking skywards. It was then that I am certain I caught God's eye; it had a twinkle in it, a look of understanding, the same quick glance I used to have with my father when we shared an unspoken joke.

Poor old God doesn't have much to joke about at the moment. He must be considering that His decision to create mankind was a bit of a mistake.

I must remember to throw a bucket of water over the Rambling Rector rose that I planted recently. It may not survive the present drought, and I am hoping I shall live long enough to see it bloom.

I need to take control of my mind before it is too late. Friends tell me that when you become a dotard, you can find solace in classical music. Having lived all my life in the shadow of Benny Goodman, and Fats Waller, I fear I may be too old to make the switch. Jazz lifts the spirits whereas classical tests the emotions and, however beautiful, may take you back to dark places that you have no wish to revisit. The start of Beethoven's Fifth reminds me of the Nazis, and the Nazis remind me of the chosen people, and the chosen people remind me what is going on at this moment between Israel and Gaza. How a people who have been so persecuted for centuries can lack compassion distresses me.

The only person with whom I could ever discuss this died of old age two years ago, even though he was younger than me. He was one of many truly wonderful men I have been privileged to meet during my life. That I was foolish enough not to marry any of them was entirely my misjudgement at the time.

I never met his daughter but she phoned me to tell me of his death, so I must have been in his address book, which is a comforting thought. His name was Frank and we met accidentally on holiday, when all the best things happen.

Hugh and I talked a lot about holidays and I tried to accommodate his interests. I declined the invitation to be part of the crew on a square rigger that he and his buddies leased to sail around the Scottish Islands to visit Kilda and North Rona. I only had to go out in a rowing boat on Ullswater in order to be sick. Instead I booked myself an expensive single ticket on one of those exclusive educational travels to the Middle East. It was the first of many to that part of the world.

I became practised at being a single woman of advancing years travelling on her own. I always took a lightweight book with me and on the first night of any expedition would find a corner in the lounge or bar, or wherever the assembly point was, and pretend to read it. It made me feel and look less alone.

On that evening, the evening I met Frank, I had just opened my book when a cultured male voice said, 'Excuse me – are you on your own?'

I said that I was.

'I am too. May I join you?'

I put down the book and looked up at my knight in shining armour. Outwardly he was a slight, insignificant man with receding white hair and glasses. He was holding what I presumed to be an alcoholic drink and he sat down and started talking.

He was recently widowed. His wife's death had come as a shock; she was a retired teacher, only seventy-five. They had booked this trip together. His children had insisted that he go through with it, thinking it would help him get over his loss, so here he was returning to a place he had known well in the past.

He offered to get me a drink. He obviously knew his way around Muslim countries. 'I wouldn't mind a whisky,' I said.

He spoke in a foreign tongue to the passing attendant.

'Do you speak the local language?' I asked.

It transpired that Frank spoke fluent Arabic having been with the British Mandate in Palestine in 1947 and 1948. He had worked in communications and was all too aware of the mistakes made by politicians that had led to the tragedy that now engulfs the Middle East. He was staunchly pro-Palestinian.

There was a spiritual dimension to him, a deep sense of faith, something Hugh never possessed because it was knocked out of him as a child. Perhaps that is why, when I think about it, I have always been attracted to men with faith. I found the same quality in Clive, the final love of my life: faith and an appreciation of a good single malt.

In Frank's company, doors opened. He was the most wonderful, knowledgeable travelling companion with whom I was only too happy to share a Bedouin tent when the time came. We lay awake, talking our way towards the desert's dawn and looking at the stars, discussing what might have been. We kept in touch for the next ten years, phoning every Sunday even though we never met up again. Now all that wisdom was gone.

It is fascinating how far the memories of music can take you; this destination arrived via the first two bars of Beethoven's Fifth.

Dear old Hugh never complained about my friendships. They probably got me out of his hair and he had his own lady friends who went with him on holiday. They were stalwart souls prepared to crew for him, who volunteered to take part in the tall-ships' races, so things evened themselves out.

Hugh was into brass bands and military music, which he played constantly in his eighties. Jazz had to take a back seat. We both shared a love of male-voice choirs; to this day, I cannot listen to them without weeping, for the sound comes from life's experiences like it does in jazz. However much I try to relate to what my grandchildren call music, it is just too noisy and discordant.

I have been told I have orthostatic hypotension, which is a great relief. I have been having a few dizzy spells and blackouts and assumed it was the whisky.

***

Connor wished Nan could have met with this old biddy; they would have enjoyed a drink together. He didn't find David Bowie too noisy; he had been useful in blocking out the sound of his parents fighting.

Connor had never heard of the British Mandate in Palestine but he'd seen the fighting between Gaza and Israel on the news and bombs being dropped, and he sort of imagined that was where Harry was.

Even so, I managed to make it to Freya's wedding in Oxford. To be at your great-granddaughter's wedding has a magic about it like no other, a feeling of disbelief that you were responsible for the whole thing.

Because of the dizzy spells, the GP had advised me not to go. 'It may put a strain on your heart,' he said. 'All weddings do that!'

As he was giving this unwelcome advice, the humour of the situation got to me and I started laughing. All I could see was the undertaker with the dicky ticker in the comedy *Hallo! Hallo!*. I assured the doctor that it was just a case of mind over matter.

The car journey down to Oxford went well. I wore an elephant-size Pamper nappy. Anna, who was doing the driving, told me beforehand that she wasn't stopping for anything and the four-and-a-half-hour drive would be non-stop. The B&B was excellent; we had decided that The Randolph was too expensive, and anyway it would be chock-a-block with Chinese tourists.

The wedding will be my last social outing, and a wonderful one on which to go out and start the slow, final, lonely, uphill struggle towards the grave. Oxford, 'the city of dreaming spires' – to experience it once more under such happy circumstances was a precious bonus. This was the place where I partied in those salad days of innocence. I remember those summer evenings at May Balls in the early months of peace in the late 1940s, and the excitement of forbidden sex still to come.

And now Freya was experiencing the magic. She walked down the aisle of St Giles wearing the diamond-and-pearl spray pendant my parents gave to me on my twenty-first birthday.

The pendant's last airing had been more than fifty years earlier in a different setting, in those glitzy, false days of corporate entertaining in New York and LA when Hugh and I were still top of the midden.

The day was glorious. There wasn't a cloud in the sky and it was almost too hot for comfort. An elderly man that I didn't know kindly took my left arm as we left the church. My stick clutched firmly in my right hand, we made the walk back to Green Templeton College, to the grounds of the Observatory where the marquee for the reception had been erected. My new companion sat me down in the shade on one of those wooden seats that encircle trees. They have a special name, but I can't remember it.

He asked, 'Are you the great-grandmother?' When that had been established, he went in search of the champagne.

I had a small flask of whisky in my handbag and was dying for a sip but thought better of it at this early stage. I didn't want to let down my side of the family, and I knew that my reputation might have gone before me.

My Good Samaritan returned with a tray and two glasses and some biscuity things topped with smoked salmon and caviar, small enough to pop into your mouth in one go. With such a delicate feast, there was no need to question why God hadn't created us with three hands or, if Darwin was right, why they hadn't evolved by now.

'You'll need a few of these,' he said. 'The sit-down meal isn't until four-thirty.' Then we talked about the day's celebrations and how the live music with full choir and organist added to the sanctity of the moment. We had both particularly enjoyed the anthem 'I Sat Down Under His Shadow' by Edward Bairstow.

'I'm a jazz man myself,' my companion said, and suddenly it seemed as if we had known one another for ever. He had met

Benny Goodman, and still travelled to New Orleans every year to the jazz festival.

We studied the schedule for the day's celebrations, which had been slipped into the Order of Service. I had already decided that it would be foolhardy to stay for the disco in the evening and far too noisy. But when we read *8pm, Souls that Swing. 11.30, Carriages* he said, 'I'm game if you are.'

Much later we were twisting again, as they did last summer, when I heard above the music one of the bridesmaids shouting to Freya, 'I see your great-gran's got off with the Lord Chief Justice!'

I had wondered who the guests might be. The wedding itself was beautifully understated – no penguin suits or top hats, lounge suits by request. Freya walked to the church on her father's arm from their home around the corner along Woodstock Road as pedestrians offered their good wishes and applause, and Chinese tourists clicked their cameras. Because of my age I was chauffeured to the church; there are advantages in being old.

***

Connor had never been to Oxford but he felt that he knew it quite well. Gloria and he often watched *Morse* and *Lewis*. He thought that the old biddy's family couldn't be all that posh because posh people always wore grey top hats at weddings. All the football stars did, too, and the royal family. They even wore toppers to go racing.

***

The Observatory had opened its doors so that those guests who needed a break from the disco and still had the energy to climb the spiral staircase to its summit could witness the sky at night. It was a myriad of stars on a backdrop of dark blue, resting on a horizon of orange glow left by the sun, a silhouette of spires in the foreground.

I felt an arm around my waist. For a second, I thought that His Honour the judge had followed me up, but this was a more familiar arm. It felt like Harry's, even though I knew it couldn't be. It had not been an option for him to take time off to attend a wedding, however much he loved his cousin; his sense of responsibility was too great. But he was there in spirit, even as he watched the sun rise over the desert. It looked bigger and brighter than the one back home. There were no dreaming spires, just a sea of grubby white tents and an ocean of despair stretching over the horizon as far as the eye could see.

I remembered Harry saying to me all those years ago when he was in his teens and becoming aware of things, 'Everything has beauty but not everyone sees it.'

I spent this morning scurryfunging, the family name for the activity that precedes an uninvited guest when you rush around trying to hide things in drawers to make the place look tidy to pacify the expectations of your visitors, and thereafter can never find anything. It was only the podiatrist coming, but I felt I should make the effort.

There comes a time when you realise that you no longer wish, nor are able, to deal with the problems of your children. It creeps up, growing stronger each year together with that ghastly feeling of guilt that you have been a rotten parent. I'd better not have a drink.

I have convinced myself that nothing good comes from technology. If I open my emails to see whether one of my grandchildren has been in touch, I will be greeted by the Dark Web with an attachment of a Bosch painting of damnation.

My grandchildren tell me I am electrically challenged – or is it electronically – and they are probably right. I can hardly tell the difference between a screw-in and a bayonet light bulb.

I have never been good at decisions. As a child I bit my fingernails and was reprimanded constantly; the bitter aloes they painted on my nails daily never worked.

***

Connor thought that he must stop biting his nails too. Most of the white boys at school did. The girls didn't bite theirs but they had anorexia instead.

***

Yesterday I went a whole day without a drink and I am feeling righteous, but this morning my body is reminding me that it was just a blip, an error of judgement. I must quickly get back to my old ways if my mind is to have any chance of survival.

I switched on Bob Dylan then looked in the fridge for something to eat. I found some old rice pudding; it is amazing how good cold rice pudding tastes when you are hungry.

I have been going through old family papers and letters. The beautiful copperplate hands from decades ago have become familiar, and I feel sometimes that their writers are in the room with me. There are letters from daughters to mothers and mothers to daughters, where they refer to their husband or father as imbibing a little too much or being a little too fond of the bottle. Now it is called alcoholism and is still hidden behind closed doors.

***

Connor remembered his dad had, on occasions, been found in the morning, still dressed in yesterday's filthy boiler suit. He would be sprawled in his chair, clutching a pack of Newcastle Brown and saying he was going to call in sick. Connor was usually late for school on those days and had to explain the situation to Miss, for she always told the class that school and home must integrate. She had become his confessor, mother and social worker, as well as yacking on about Shakespeare.

In one of the lessons, they had discussed drink in that 'do goodie' way lefties had of making you feel guilty. 'Drinking is a social problem,' Miss had said.

Fuck that, thought Connor. It's the only way my Dad can cope with life. But he also understood that that was why his Asian and Afro-Caribbean classmates, who sat on the front row and whose parents had religious convictions, had done better than him.

Miss had continued, 'Being drunk brings out the best and worst in people. It can tear down inhibitions and give your mind a false sense of freedom. The Lakeland poets are a perfect example. Without drugs and alcohol, they probably wouldn't have been so creative. But it can also remind you of who you really are and unleash your dark side.'

***

Sunday mornings have become guilt ridden. My mind is tut-tutting, or is it something deeper? Am I trying to hold onto something I no longer believe in, those childhood certainties that good would eventually triumph because it made everyone feel better when everything around us was saying there wasn't a chance in hell of that happening? I don't want to burden my grandchildren with this dilemma.

It was Harry working with the dispossessed who was so insistent that I carry my mobile with me at all times in case of emergencies, but I lose it constantly. I can hear it pinging from goodness knows where. I think it must be in the bedroom and I climb the stairs yet again. They have become my Mount Everest, the half landing the base camp where I stop for breath in order to make the final assault.

When I get to the top, I flop down onto the bed and pull the duvet over me, feeling the blissful comfort and reassurance of the mattress, and I try to remember why I came upstairs in the first place. Sometimes I start to take off my jeans, thinking it is bedtime.

Someone told me recently that I look good in jeans – well, not in so many words. What they actually said was, 'There are not many women in their nineties who can get away with wearing jeans.'

Why is it the moment you get upstairs someone knocks on the door? The banging was persistent, probably the pharmacy with the repeat prescription, eyedrops for my glaucoma, directions on the package which say: *Knock very loudly, patient very deaf.*

You must never make a quick descent of Everest because it is more hazardous than the ascent. Make certain that the grab rail is firmly in your grasp before you allow either of your feet to make a move, and try to ignore the persistent banging. Usually I shout 'Come in' at the top of my voice but my voice no longer carries. Once upon a time I could jump from the top of a flight of stairs to the bottom when my brothers challenged me to do so.

It wasn't the chemist but the nice, smiley local greengrocer who presented me with a bunch of assorted blooms. There were four roses amongst them. I bent forward to smell them, but they had no scent.

I remember saying that it wasn't my birthday, have you got the wrong address? And I thought, well, whoever it is at least they've had the common sense not to send me a teddy bear, which seems to be all the rage nowadays even amongst adults. No one rushed around bearing teddy bears during the Blitz. I've seen them in graveyards alongside flowers rotting and sweating in their cellophane; why on earth does anyone need a teddy bear when they are dead?

'It's Mother's Day,' the greengrocer said and handed me the card tucked inside the cellophane. It read: *On Mother's Day, thanks for being there, lots of love from us all. The children, grandchildren and great-grandchildren.*

I should have been grateful, but I felt a resentment. I didn't want to be reminded of my middle life, for I have convinced myself that I got motherhood wrong. I have now, just about, come to terms with my mistakes and reached a certain peace of mind.

And it wasn't just that, it was the profligacy of that act of kindness. Surely my family know I have a garden full of roses, old-fashioned roses with delicious scents that come forward to greet you as you walk towards them. I have no need of force-fed blooms which come with instructions on how to keep them alive. Cut off in their prime, made to travel halfway round the world, wrapped in polythene, their chemical succour in a pouch Sellotaped to their stems, after a brief sojourn with me they are destined for the dustbin. When I was younger they went on the compost heap, but I am no longer allowed to go out on my own because of the dizzy spells.

I have never fully understood Mother's Day. I accept Mothering Sunday as a Christian celebration to glorify the mother of our Lord, but it wasn't meant to be a commercial bonanza for the high street and Amazon.

Whenever I am doubtful and suspicious about the motives of others, I listen to Bob Dylan. I have just turned him on and he is singing that he can hear a sweet voice calling and it must be the mother of our Lord.

I looked up at the poster stuck with Blutac on the wall above my computer. It is *The Annunciation* by Fra Angelico, which I had enlarged at vast expense from a postcard bought in Florence in those distant, heady days of holidays in Italy. Mary is sitting on what looks like a three-legged stool, her arms in submission as she is approached by the angel Gabriel to give her a warning of what she and the whole of womankind are letting themselves in for.

When I was little, I had a three-legged stool. It was kept in the corner of the cow byre and at milking time I would sit on it and milk the cow, my head tucked into her soft warm flanks as I squeezed her teats, the milk making a reassuring squirting sound as it joined the frothy warm milk in the pail.

Of course, you are no longer allowed to say 'woman-kind'; it has to be 'person kind' otherwise you could be arrested for discrimination or something. I looked up Mothering Sunday on the internet and it appears the ancient Greeks and Romans got there first. They were holding festivals for the mother goddesses Rhea and Cybele centuries before Mary came on the scene. Now it has turned into tacky cards and withering flowers – and I, if I'm not careful, will turn into a curmudgeon.

***

Connor wondered what a curmudgeon was. He had a problem pronouncing it in his head. There were other words the old biddy used which he didn't understand; somewhere she had called herself a dotard, and what did sojourn mean? He rummaged in his top drawer and found the biro with which he had attempted to finish his homework and scribbled the words down in an old exercise book.

***

The Best of Dylan has just turned itself off. Harry gave me the CD a few Christmases ago when he sensed I was ready for it. He knew I would prefer it to lavender-scented talcum powder. It is already feeling its age and has developed hiccups from overuse.

Harry texted me to say he will send me a new one via Amazon – or should it have read via the Amazon? Geography was my favourite subject at school. I was awarded a gold star once for an essay on the indigenous peoples of the Amazon basin – were they pygmies, or was that the Belgian Congo?

It was Hugh's birthday yesterday, the fifteenth of March, the Ides of March. Pretty prophetic. He would have been 110 years old and we would have been celebrating seventy-five years of uneasy togetherness had he not popped his clogs more than a decade ago. His passing has allowed my mind to range freely.

Why does the civilised world make such a fuss about dying? All those quandaries about who to ask to act as your attorney when your solicitor thinks you are going barmy. Animals don't need powers of attorney and they are of far more value to the planet than mankind. Civilised world: a misnomer if ever there was one.

I have to admit that old age has come upon me overnight and I am still not a true believer in the eyes of the established church just when I need to be. Faith is a different matter because it is in the air you breathe. I must have been a bit of a disappointment to those who taught me the catechism at far too tender an age.

You cannot teach faith, just as you cannot teach people and races to love one another by passing laws. Darwin was correct on one level: love evolves from understanding and respect.

Litre bottles of Bell's and Famous Grouse are on offer this week and Bacchus is in need of a knees-up. Of course, I am now dependent upon Stella delivering it without tutting. But I should have known her better; she winked and said, 'Here's your necessary. You're over twenty-five, aren't you? It's rather heavy. I'll put my mask on and put it on the kitchen table for you.'

A few hours later I switched on Bob Dylan 'Hey, Mr Tambourine Man'. He is telling me to forget about today until tomorrow. Let me forget about today until tomorrow.

My old cheap Woolies' alarm clock has given up the ghost. Initially I thought it was the battery, but it isn't. I shall rely on the grandfather clock striking the hour. At my age, the minutes no longer matter and it would be a waste of money to buy a new one. Anyway, I am very unlikely to oversleep for my bladder, my old adversary, will come to the rescue and rouse me.

I have decided to spend a constructive day going through my books. I can't bear the thought that they may be destined for the skip when I kick the bucket. The house is full of them; the bookcases are overflowing and there are small mountains of unsteady piles in the corners of almost every room, waiting to be gone through. Once upon a time they had value. I was fortunate to get a decent price for Hugh's old books but that was a decade ago and he never read fiction, just authoritative books about military conquests which some specialist in Edinburgh found interesting and was happy to take off my hands.

The pile in the spare room, which guests have tolerated for six decades, has just collapsed. The books have scattered into a fan shape across the floor. They are mainly from my childhood,.

I couldn't believe it – *Little Black Sambo*, the hero of my youth! There he was, face upwards, dressed in his familiar red jacket and purple trousers and Mother was reading to me again.

I interrupted her and said, 'When I am grown up, I am going to marry Little Black Sambo.'

She had replied without hesitation, 'Are you, darling? How nice. But Africa is such a long, long way away. Daddy and I would miss you. And you know how insects make a beeline for you and you come out in those nasty blebs. Africa is full of insects.'

Of course, I married Hugh, though I wouldn't have minded the insects.

***

Connor's nan had a copy of *Little Black Sambo.* He had once mentioned it to Miss, but she said it was discriminatory and racist and he mustn't read it.

CHAPTER 5

Today Poppy came. I was sitting in the garden watching the bees pollinating, when someone I didn't recognise came round the corner of the house. She was tall, beautiful, mid-thirtyish and carrying a bunch of flowers. My first thought was for the flowers. Why had anyone felt it necessary to cut them off in their prime? I shall have to get up and find a vase and some water for them.

'It's Poppy – Patricia. You must remember.'

I didn't but I said, 'Yes, of course—'

'It's been such a long time – how wonderful that you remember. You were so kind in allowing my sister and me to pitch our tent in the paddock. My sister, her children and I are staying at a campsite near Ullswater, and I felt I must just pop over and say hello.'

'How kind of you. If you go into the house Poppy – Polly – dear, I think there is a jug on the draining board by the sink for the flowers.'

My memory is in three recognisable parts, rather like a sandwich: childhood and the dotage in which I now live are two slices of wholesome bread but middle age, its filling, has at times been unpalatable. Like motherhood, it was a time when I felt I got nothing right. And here is a ghost from the past to bring it all back.

I sat back in the wicker garden chair with its comforting cushions, which a kind neighbour has lent me for the summer, and tried to remember. Polly was going on about something – or did she say she was Poppy? All I could hear were the bumble bees buzzing from stamen to stamen carrying their yellow cargo.

If only I'd had the courage to believe in myself in those middle years I might remember. I might not be afraid of myself when it is others of whom I should be afraid. Why on earth am I now being made to feel guilty by someone, who, as a child spent a few days in a tent in the paddock? I should feel flattered that she remembers that long ago I gave her something in her childhood to treasure, to hold on to. But it cost me dear.

I remember now. Hugh was unwelcoming; in fact, he was downright unpleasant. 'I don't want other people's kids on my land.'

'Shush, they'll hear. They are just small children having an adventure.'

'I don't bloody care! Get them off.'

Truths come, but not always at a convenient time.

I held my ground. It had not been the right time to remind Hugh that it was not his land but my land, not that there would ever be a right time for he would never have understood. He lived in the joyless world of possessions. But beneath the surface lay an honourable man, shackled by an unhappy childhood. His irascibility, his dislike and mistrust of the human race were fixed during his early years.

Above the sound of the bees and Polly is chattering, the grandfather clock in the kitchen struck twelve. I had left the back door open so its mellow chimes reached the garden, reminding me that there had been some good times in those middle years.

I thought about clocks tick-tocking their way through people's lives, assured of their immortality, capable of going on forever as long as there is someone to wind them up and service them from time to time.

The first clock to enter my life had a squat round black body with a white face the size of a saucer, with three legs, and hands in the forms of Mickey and Minnie Mouse. The significance of grandfather clocks was brought home to me when I married. In my childhood home there must have been grandfather clocks in almost every room, but they went unnoticed. They were part of the furniture, looked after by someone else, not wanting to make a statement but just chiming reassurance. Time doesn't matter when you are young. You are certain you will live for ever, but then you wake up one morning feeling old and ask yourself, 'Was that it?'

Polly is still reminiscing – or did she say her name was Poppy? I can't hear a word she is saying because my hearing aid is on the kitchen table, but she sounds and looks happy, so that's okay. Perhaps I should offer her a drink of some sort, but I really can't be bothered to get up and I cannot get the grandfather clocks out of my head.

I had been assured by Hugh that the clock he brought to our marriage was very valuable. It had been with his family for yonks and was the cause of sibling friction and avarice on the death of my mother-in-law. I disliked it because of all that angst, and also because it overwhelmed the small sitting room of our first modest home. The brass bobble on the top had to be removed. Its casing is an unattractive reddish-raw mahogany and it requires polishing, and I am not houseproud. Its chime is sharp and metallic. It has been an unwelcome guest in my home for more than seventy years and now it has become a burden. Every Sunday morning it needs to be rewound and my weak, aged arms struggle to pull up its original leaden weights. I feel guilty about this, for it was crafted with love around 1790 by one William Tickle Senior of Newcastle.

Now the grandfather clock in the kitchen I love to bits, for it was brought to my home by an unexpected act of kindness. It was when the children were little – no, that isn't true. Anna was little but the others were in their teens and away at school. Hugh was on one of those lengthy overseas business trips, flying the flag for British industry and picking up the Queen's Awards for Exports, and I had been left to hold the fort.

Halfway through mowing the lawn, I somehow managed to flood the carburettor on the old Atco mowing machine and I couldn't restart it. I knew that if I wasn't very careful feelings of inadequacy would overwhelm me, and the black dog of gloom would visit again and settle on me.

An answer to an ad placed in the local newsagent's, beseeching someone to come and help in the garden, brought immediate response. I had given the address and locals knew the house. That evening Arthur knocked on the front door. Initially I thought he was an elderly tramp seeking a cup of tea. His herringbone-tweed greatcoat reached his ankles and was encased in a hessian potato sack in which a hole had been cut, whence his head appeared. The sack was held in place by a piece of string, the kind they use to tie bales of hay, and on it were the words Skelmersdale Potatoes. Although the weather was mild, he wore a balaclava and a flat cap. His gnarled fingers were visible through holes in his gloves.

He spoke politely and gently. 'I hope I haven't come at an inconvenient time, madam.' I had never in my life aspired to the title 'madam'. 'But I've just seen your note in the newsagent's window about help in the garden. I thought I would come straight away because I know the house.'

I invited him into the hall. He removed his hat and balaclava and told me his name was Arthur. He was seventy-eight years old and had been made to retire because of his age. He had been a linesman on the railways, a life spent outside in all weathers keeping the tracks clear. His wife had died four years ago, his grown-up family was in Australia, and the solitude of his small railway cottage and not being able to work outside was getting him down.

I employed him on the spot. What else could I do? I felt pity for him, and it was what my mother would have done. I have spent a lifetime helping lame dogs over stiles, and many of them have rewarded me by returning years later to say thank you. Of course, there have been those who had fallen by the wayside…

My plans for a young man capable of getting the mower started went by the board. I decided not to mention any of this to Hugh. I could contact him in some embassy or other should there be a real emergency, but I was uncertain what he would consider to be a real emergency other than me dropping down dead. And I already knew what he would say about Arthur: 'I am sick of your bloody lame ducks! You know nothing about him.'

I mentioned the lawn mower to Arthur. He asked where it was and had it going within five minutes. He said he would come twice a week, and so he did for the next six years. Hugh sensed that he might have met his match, and I had a brief, rare sense of being emboldened. Over the years, Hugh became quite fond of Arthur.

Arthur never came inside the house, even in blizzard conditions when drips from his nose had turned to icicles. He would never accept a hot cup of coffee indoors, saying, 'I don't feel the cold, I'm used to it. Since I was fourteen I've worked outside in all weathers. It's when I get too hot that I feel ill.'

One day Arthur was late arriving. I looked out of the window, concerned that he may be ill, and saw him walking up the drive pushing a hand cart with something large on it covered with a tarpaulin. I went out to meet him. He was breathless but he managed to say that he hoped I wouldn't be offended. His old hands were struggling to untie the ropes that held the object onto the cart. When he lifted the tarpaulin, there lay a grandfather clock, its beautiful painted face to the sky, its oak casing inlaid with mellowed mahogany. The base bore witness to a hard life spent on damp flagstones in the company of rats.

'Could you give my old clock a home?' Arthur asked. 'It belonged to my grandfather. I don't want to put it in a sale, I want it to go to someone who will love it. I thought of you and your husband.'

I remember wanting to cry and asking why he could no longer give it a home. It transpired that he had been found wandering in the street by a stranger and had been unable to remember where he lived. Social services were called and from then on, from Arthur's point of view, it had all been downhill.

The clock would not be welcome in the care home.

He died a week later. At his funeral, I discovered his surname was Leadbetter. There were no mourners other than a representative from social services.

Hugh mourned him in a different way; he restored part of the clock's lower casing and the plinth on which it stood. His efforts were worthy but, as he remarked, he couldn't compete with the mastery and skill of one John Wignall of Ormskirk in 1779.

I suspect that family squabbles may arise over this clock when I die.

Goodness, Polly-Poppy is still talking and I haven't heard a word. By the tone of her voice, she is upset about something.

Now I am listening; she is talking about her father.

His face was in the newspapers during the sixties, a nameless, shadowy figure in the background at international peace conferences, standing behind the well-known faces of world leaders. He was a brilliant interpreter; it was through him that ideas, suggestions, concessions and suspicions flowed. He could sense by the tone of the voices whether people were being sincere or not, and his mind filtered out misunderstandings. On his interpretations, World Treaties were signed.

On his retirement, when all around were receiving gongs and being honoured publicly, Polly's father, who had contributed so much to the understanding between nations and world peace, had somehow been left off the list. And here was his daughter, sitting in my garden with all that history and a sense of injustice festering in her mind, asking the question why. Had the media got hold of a rumour and questioned his allegiance, destroyed a reputation? They are very good at that sort of thing.

Now fully conscious of Polly-Poppy's presence, and aware that resentment is best put to one side, I said, 'So it has always been, dear. Perhaps it is easier to forgive and forget when it is you who is the victim of injustice than to witness the suffering of injustice in those you love.'

Resentment destroys you in the end. I told her of the evening Hugh returned home from work. He had been asked to clear his desk, the executive way of telling you that you are fired, but no one would – or could – tell him why. I had assured myself that it was my fault: I had failed as a diplomat, cook or host when entertaining high-powered business colleagues, said something indiscreet to a trusted company wife.

As family man Hugh was a bit of a disaster, but as a businessman he was honest and honourable. I suppose that is why I always stuck by him and convinced myself that it must have been something I had done. But good had come out of that episode. We both decided that we were no longer prepared to live out our lives beholden to others; from then on, we would go it alone.

I suppose it was the children who suffered most from the change in lifestyle but for me it was empowering. And the bonus was that I met, albeit a bit late in the day, the real loves of my life, Clive and cattle.

Connecting again with the present and instantly regretting it, I said to Poppy-Polly, 'There are a smattering of OBEs in my family,' quickly adding, 'known by all as Other Bugger's Efforts.'

We talked a little longer. As she got up to leave, she gave me a long hug and surprised me by saying, 'I have always looked upon you as my surrogate mother.' She said she would come again. She never did.

Staying in the garden, enjoying the warmth of the sun, I thought how much I had needed to hear that. My nose got sunburnt. How kind my dear neighbours are; this chair they have lent me for the summer is bliss. This chair is woven wicker and waterproof, its soft, removable cushions encouraging me to close my eyes and drift back to places I once visited in my childhood as I listened to bedtime stories. Is the Thief of Bagdad still on his magic carpet, flying above that war-ravaged place?

Even with cushions you couldn't dream on one of those hard wooden deckchairs that had belonged to Hugh's parents. He had insisted we needed no others.

And then there was Aqaba. I can't remember what year that was. My memories don't come in chronological order but are like folded blankets stored in the linen cupboards, to be shaken out when needed, releasing the odd clothes moth and destructive grub.

Aqaba was no daydream; it was real.

Of course, I knew all about T.E. Lawrence. My father had talked about him, had met him once. They were of the same generation, shared a passion for motorbikes – and there was that film. I never dreamt that one day, quite by chance, I would be sitting with a double whisky in my hand on the private beach of a swanky hotel in Aqaba thanks to modern-day pirates. They were young, passionate Somali lads carrying Kalashnikovs, intercepting oil tankers, cruise liners and yachts as they made their way north across the Indian Ocean, holding them to ransom before they could reach the Red Sea. It was retaliation; the pirates were claiming a bounty for the despoilment of their villages and ancestral fishing grounds by the oil companies and tourist industry. I had secretly lifted my glass of whisky to them and later I wanted to thank them for the diversion.

The yacht, which our small party of eight was due to board to take us down the Red Sea, up the Suez Canal and along to Cyrenaica, was waylaid. The crew were held at gunpoint until cash was handed over and the travel company obliged to find alternative accommodation for its clients. The birthplace of Simon of Cyrene would have to wait.

Having spent the past ten days in Syria and Jordan sleeping in Bedouin tents, our wardrobes were ill equipped to deal with Western standards of casual smart. Everyone else in the hotel was dressed in clean clothes. Making my way to the bar, I began to feel just as Lawrence must have felt when he returned from the desert, gasping for a drink.

***

Connor hadn't a clue what she was talking about. He didn't know where or what Aqaba was, and the only Lawrence he'd heard about was called Stephen and had been stabbed on the streets of London. His nan had wept at the news and told him how the Irish were made unwelcome when they moved to Glasgow. When they sought lodgings, the signs in boarding-house windows said: *VACANCIES, NO COLOUREDS, IRISH OR DOGS.* It was razors rather than knives that the gangs carried then, the Protestant Billy Boys and the Catholic Norman Conks.

He had intended to ration his time on the computer but he started to wonder – was Aqaba in Syria? The old biddy had mentioned that Harry was in Syria. Could there be a connection? A thought struck him: had Harry read any of this? Could he, Connor, be the only person who has ever seen it?

***

I awoke with such enthusiasm for the day ahead after four hours of sleep with no nightmares to turn day into night, and only three interruptions from my bladder demanding attention.

I am trying very hard not to think about care homes, old peoples' homes and the inevitability of my sell-by date. I shouldn't have turned on Bob Dylan and been reminded of that dark, descending cloud and been asked how it feels to be on my own.

In Aqaba he was on his own, just as I was. Hugh would have called him one of my lame dogs. He was a middle-aged Japanese man who had kept himself to himself throughout the ten-day expedition to explore ancient archaeological sites. Perhaps he sensed hostility from his travelling companions. That evening he had seated himself at a side table for two in the dining room, whilst the rest of the group sat at a table in the middle of the room.

The courier had told them that the Japanese gentleman would not be continuing with them. His early-morning flight home was booked from Sharm el Sheik. I had suggested that on that final night we should ask him to join us, but insufficient time had elapsed since the madness and misunderstandings of the war and reconciliation was not high on the party's agenda. Memories were still raw and forgiveness a long way off. It was too soon for some people to turn the other cheek.

Sometimes memories are best left alone and allowed to wither on the vine, for they can become the conveyer belt of guilt. But sometimes, just sometimes, it is important not to let go.

'Well, if you won't bury the hatchet I will.' I left prejudice and my hors d'oeuvre at the table.

As I walked away, I heard someone say, 'Stupid woman.'

I approached the Japanese man's table and asked if I might join him. He rose, gave a small bow and pulled back the empty chair. He spoke perfect English. To keep things light, I asked him whether he had enjoyed sleeping in a tent under the stars.

'Yes, but I sensed the hostility. I have learnt to keep my distance. I understand it.'

'War brings out the best and worst in people,' I said.

'That's what I write about.'

'You're an author?'

'Yes. There are no winners in war.'

As the waiter transferred my place setting to his table, I started to tell him about my husband. Towards the end of the war, when Hugh was twenty-one, he was with the British Pacific Fleet serving on an aircraft carrier. His great friend was killed just feet away from him by a Kamikaze plane. A fleeting glimpse of terror in the eyes of the Japanese pilot was frozen into Hugh's memory. 'He was just a young lad like me,' he would often say.

After the atom bombs and the Japanese surrender, there was the repatriation back to Sydney of the Australian prisoners of war from the death camps. Row upon row of skeletal bodies, smoking fags and cracking jokes and praying for the strength to make it back to Sydney. They knew full well, though, that before sunrise many of their comrades would have been slipped into the ocean and consumed by the waves from beneath the Australian flag, their digger hats left behind on deck to be taken home to loved ones. It was those images that Hugh could not erase.

My dining companion was silent for a while. Then he said, 'Let me tell you about my beloved younger brother. He was a civil engineering graduate from Tokyo University. He hoped to become a great bridge builder, emulating your Brunel, but after Pearl Harbour he was conscripted into the Imperial Army. He was sent to Burma with other graduates to oversee the building of a bridge over the river Mae Kong. After the war he was tried for war crimes and executed. He was twenty-four. Understanding and decency rotted into the ground, like the unharvested rice at home.'

We talked into the night. The others had gone to bed, casting disapproving glances as they left the dining room, and the waiters were looking impatient.

My Japanese friend's name was Kazuo. He said, 'In my room I have something I would like you to take home to your husband.'

I followed him to his room. He offered me a drink from the fridge and then opened his backpack. He took out a book and asked for Hugh's full name, then he sat down at the desk and wrote something on the flyleaf. I saw that he was weeping.

I have never been attracted to men of oriental hue or features, but that night I would willingly have slept with the enemy had there been an invitation.

CHAPTER 6

Connor remembered his granddad hadn't liked the Japs either; it was a wartime thing.

Oh God, he could feel a stiffy coming on. He was trying hard to adapt to their unpredictability but they came upon him at the most inconvenient times. The first one was when Gloria arrived and gave him a great big motherly hug and called him pet. Could this one be because he had read the words 'sleeping with the enemy'? Dad had not explained things all that well.

It dawned on him that you could be aroused by other people's thoughts. All those girls who Seb got off with were wasting a lot of time and money on false eyelashes and mascara to catch his attention. Connor knew he was no Brad Pitt – freckles and red hair didn't turn girls on – but even so they tried it on with him. He knew they did it to embarrass him and make him feel stupid, egging him on to the point of no return, giggling then walking away.

He wished he'd paid more attention to that girl in the front row in class who wore a brace and always got high marks. Seb had made fun of her because of the brace and called her a swot.

***

That book burnt a hole in my luggage for the rest of the trip. Kazuo had put it in an envelope addressed to Hugh and sealed it. Much as I was tempted to take a peek to see what was written on the flyleaf, I respected his wishes. For the time being, it was for Hugh's eyes only.

I would have enjoyed my Japanese friend's companionship in Cyrenia; he would have been in tune with a place devoid of war, not on the tourist trail, and yet to be restored, developed and despoiled for the tourist trade. Wildflowers filled the crevices between the foundation stones where once there had been mortar cementing an earlier civilisation. They made a patchwork of colour and scent, criss-crossing as far as the eye could see, accompanied by the continuous humming of bees collecting their nectar.

Two thousand years ago Simon of Cyrene might have played as a child in this enchanted place, little knowing that one day he would help a stranger carry His cross.

A couple of young shepherd boys were tending their flocks amongst the flowers, taking time off to gather the honey from the bees' secret places, oblivious to their stings. They offered it from their cupped hands as refreshment to passers-by in exchange for a small coin.

I dipped my finger in and I tasted the nectar of the gods. Licking my fingers clean, I searched in my purse for a coin. There was a collection of the remnants of travel from different countries of various denominations. I fished out two and, not knowing their value, gave them to one of the shepherds. Catching his eye, I sensed that he did. A smile crossed his face, and I don't think I imagined the twinkle in his eye.

That was many years ago. I imagine them now, young men no longer offering succour, necklaces of ammunition draped across their fine young bodies, militarised by Western intervention. The women probably still offer honey in old, discarded jars to the occasional tourist, the crystallised bees in it making sure that, should it arrive at Heathrow, it wouldn't have a hope in hell of getting through security.

I did not enjoy Malta, the last stop before my final flight. It was far too crowded, but I did manage to queue up for half a day in the Cathedral without my bladder playing up, shuffling past the Caravaggios to catch a fleeting glimpse of John the Baptist being decapitated. It wasn't the happiest way to end a lifetime of travel.

***

What the hell is a Caravaggio, Connor thought. He had heard of John the Baptist – Nan had mentioned him once or twice – but he hadn't clue who he was. He sometimes wished he was back in school and could put his hand up, but he knew that from now on he would have to find out things for himself.

Miss had always said, 'When you leave school, don't feel it is the end of learning and our friendship. You can contact me any time.' But Connor was streetwise and knew that if he did, nosey suspicious neighbours fed by a salacious media would be only too happy to turn his evening visits into something else, and he didn't want to get Miss into trouble.

***

I arrived home in pouring rain to my beloved Cumbrian fells with a feeling of elation and the certainty that the definition in the Oxford dictionary of coincidence as 'mere chance' was way off course. Coincidence is intertwined with faith and fate – the three are a trinity.

Remembering the book in my luggage, I told Hugh I had a present for him. I sensed he was expecting a piece of papyrus with a touristy cliché of good wishes on it. I said, 'I met this interesting Japanese writer and he asked me to give you this book.'

Hugh looked at me closely and refused to take it, saying, 'There are no nice Japanese.' Later I put it in his study in the hope that his curiosity might one day get the better of him.

An eye for an eye, a tooth for a tooth was Hugh's mandate; he didn't understand 'love thy neighbour' or 'forgive us our trespasses as we try to forgive those who trespass against us'. I find it difficult, for the Bible seems to send out mixed messages and it is easy to become confused. I wonder whether the Koran might explain things more simply.

Memory is such a two-edged sword. That reconnection with mind and body of long ago can bring such immeasurable joy; when you remember things that have gone right, it can send you on a high of ecstasy. But there have been times when I got things wrong. Then memory is cruel and clever, arousing me from uneasy sleep with dreams of such vividness that I awake sweating to relive them again.

A recurring nightmare was of myself as a child doing something in innocence but it being witnessed through adult eyes; night after night the dream came, making me go downstairs to pour a double whisky at 6.30am and switch on Bob Dylan's 'Don't Think Twice It's All Right'.

There is no one left to ask, to verify things for me. I have outlived two of my three beloved brothers. Now there is only David at the end of a phone to share memories and bear witness, to be silly with for half an hour every Sunday morning, to reminisce with instead of going to church. We still greet each other in Cumbrian dialect.

'Hoo'sta gaan on, sis?' David says.

'Champion,' I reply, unless I am feeling under the weather, when it is, 'Nobbut middlin.'

David could bear witness to my spanking, for I had proudly shown the imprint of Mother's hand on my bottom to my brothers the following day. It had been a rite of passage.

I came across Mother's strong hand again the other day as I was going through papers that should have been dealt with half a century ago. She wasn't all spanking and discipline; she also wrote limericks about people in the village, sang songs to us that she had learnt from her father:

'There was an old man named Michael Finnegan
He had whiskers on his chin-a-gen—'

***

'Along came the wind and blew them in again.
Poor old Michael Finnegan, begin again.'
Connor was singing at the top of his voice. It was one of his Nan's songs. How he wished he could hug the old biddy.

***

As well as dealing with the discipline, Mother had a fun side to her. Father was the physical one: he stroked, caressed, sympathised and forgave, and took us on treats. In a way, it was one of those treats – a trip to the circus – that created the misunderstanding and led to the unjust spanking.

Bertram Mills Circus. Father always chose the best seats, a safe distance from the clowns which he knew scared me. Looking back, I can't really remember the animals. I know there were prancing white horses and lions in cages and men in top hats cracking whips. Then the lights went out and the marquee was in darkness. A roll of drums heralded an eerie green light focused on the centre of the ring. The programme said: *Fire and Water – Korda The Amazing Crocodile Lady.*

Even now I can remember my terror. A huge water tank had replaced the sawdust and on the bottom, completely submerged, lay a brown lady with frizzy black hair. She was wearing what looked like a swimming costume made of fish scales – and two crocodiles were swimming around her.

For five minutes, I watched in horror. I don't remember standing up and shouting, 'She's going to drown and be eaten,' but my brothers assured me that I did just that. Hugely embarrassed, they pulled me back into my seat saying, 'Sit down, you idiot.'

Suddenly the brown lady arose like Venus, mounted one of the crocodiles and waved to the crowds. A fire was now encircling the tank. Dismounting, she climbed down a small ladder attached to the outside of the tank just as the flames turned to glowing embers. Then she walked on them; you could hear her body sizzling.

On the way home my brothers called me a sissy. Father said, 'Now nobody is to try any tricks like that at home.'

'You know, if you walk quickly enough through a bed of nettles they don't sting you. It's the same with fire,' David said.

Of course, the following day my brothers suggested the nettle test. We took off our clothes and ran naked very quickly through a large clump of nettles – and we didn't get stung.

Eager to share this newfound knowledge with friends, we cycled down to the village and brought some of them back with us. There was a younger child who was being a bit chicken; I picked her up from behind, my hands under her armpits, and swung her at speed through the nettles. It was unfortunate that the child's mother witnessed this. Although the child was laughing with pleasure, it was seen as an act of cruel bullying and reported to Mother.

The spanking happened that evening as I stood in the bath.

The reason given was that I had been unkind to another child, and I realised that from then on that that was how Mother would see me. Mother never forgave; she bore grudges, and she could wring a chicken's neck without giving it a thought. Father forgave just about anything.

***

Blimey, thought Connor, she's saying things like she's writing what Miss would call a memoir.

He knew how it felt to be misunderstood, and he wished he could have given the old biddy a hug. He had been at the receiving end of numerous unjust cuffs around the ears from his real mum. Once, when his ears were red and swollen, Miss had remarked on them.

Connor was upset. He was growing to love his old biddy, and the fact that she had been unhappy made him sad. The thought that she had carried her particular unhappiness for so long worried him.

He was gradually realising that these were not just the jottings of some barmy old bat but someone who was trying to put her life down on paper, wanting to be heard before it was too late. Just as he had with Nan, he had become her listener. Had anyone else read this stuff, or had she kept it secret as he did with his own thoughts?

He didn't know how much more was on the hard drive, but now he was looking forward to it. He realised that it was holding more of his attention than Twitter and Instagram.

Had her grandson Harry read it before it was thrown out?

And she was still talking…

***

The most amusing and bizarre thing happened today. It really started yesterday with a phone call I thought was a hoax. I don't usually reach the phone in time – fourteen rings does not give me sufficient time to find the handset, which I never appear to have to hand.

A voice said, 'This is the Russian Embassy. Tomorrow an attaché will be visiting you to present you with a posthumous medal for Hugh.'

I honestly thought that someone was taking the mickey, that Hugh was somehow conniving to get back into my orbit, unsettling my widowhood with his presence and reminding me that once he had been that dashing young naval officer whom I had loved so passionately. The officer who had spent his twenty-first birthday on the Arctic convoys, on 'the worst journey in the world' as Churchill put it.

An hour ago I was sitting in a secluded part of the garden, undressed for sunbathing, when a young man appeared. He had tried knocking at the door; getting no reply he had, with Russian determination, sought me out.

He was charming and introduced himself as Olaf, an attaché instructed by Putin to make a formal presentation. I found it quite difficult to keep a straight face as a photo was taken, with my scraggy old body exposed for the world to see. But when I think about it now, I suppose the Russians are in need of some good international publicity at the moment.

CHAPTER 7

I am having problems with my mind. Memories and imagination are proving difficult bedfellows, stirring things up that have lain dormant for so long, making me feel that 'I have done those things which I ought not to have done and there is no health in me'. Guilt, that old adversary of childhood is coming to the fore.

I am being taken back to a time when things felt better but probably were not. When imagination was Peter Pan and Wendy, little Jesus meek and mild and Incy Wincy Spider.

Incy Wincy spider
Climbed up the water spout.
Down came the rain
And washed poor Incy out.
Out came the sun
And dried up all the rain,
So Incy Wincy spider
Climbed up the spout again

Why am I, yet again, writing all this rubbish down on my computer as though it were going to be of some importance to someone someday? Why am I regurgitating my thoughts every five minutes? Perhaps it is because those closest to me won't listen.

Mankind has become too clever by half and now those in

charge are not going to allow those who think differently to climb the spout again. Like sea-snot, the wokes are multiplying fast; what they say goes, however irrational. They have woven a web of human rights, capturing and destroying all that once was good, cocooning it in the sticky substance of sentimentality.

It has been the same in the village since the new houses were built and snapped up by those wanting a second home in the countryside. With no knowledge of the village's historic drainage system and no plans available, the Planning Authority gave permission for the development. It would boost the tourist trade, they said.

The only person who had knowledge of these things, and who carried the plans in his head, was an old fellow called Jack and he died years ago. He understood septic tanks and knew when the bacteria needed replacing. For centuries there were no problems and the small septic tank served the community faithfully; now nasty things are happening. That which had been flushed away is returning and houses and yards are being flooded.

***

Gosh, thought Connor, that's really interesting. He wanted to tell his dad all about it. He stopped reading and sat on the edge of his bed, wondering what he should do. The first thing was to make a note of the things he had read about but didn't understand. What was a Caravaggio? It sounded sort of Italian, like a pizza.

He decided to make written notes rather than put them on his smartphone. He looked in a drawer and found a pencil; it had a rubber attached to one end so he could rub things out if he made a mistake.

***

Perhaps that's why I love Fred Astaire singing 'Pick yourself up, dust yourself down and start all over again'. The trouble is that my mind would love the chance, but my body has vetoed any suggestion of it. I shall have that song played at my funeral just to remind people what fun life once was and still can be.

In my early teens, I made a false promise. Coached in the catechism to get the answers right, I had commitment and belief imposed upon me by the laying on of the kind hands of the then Bishop of St Asaph. The Holy Trinity, that mystical communion of Heaven knows what, urged my teenage mind to believe in something that did not appear to exist. The Bible screamed original sin and here I am, all these years later, screaming with it.

That woman in the garden of Eden did not just nibble at the apple, she took a bloody great bite even though she had been warned against it. Thank God I was never put in the position of being responsible for the waywardness of all of mankind, womankind and transgender kind. Worrying about the family is bad enough.

I started humming to Bob Dylan, his lyrics in my head. He is telling me to go at my own chosen speed. For now it is Bob Dylan to whom I listen, although I catch God's eye from time to time. If I stand in a certain place in the kitchen and look up through the second window pane on the left, He is there on the summit of Crossfell, just above the outcrop of rock where snow collects in drifts in the winter and stays until spring. One year the snow was still attracting late skiers in the summer, whilst down in the valley our neighbours were clipping sheep and making hay.

I caught His eye again this morning and thought I saw a

tear. I tell my disbelieving friends this, for it is important to keep the rumour of God's existence alive. They look at me and convince themselves that I am senile.

***

Reading this, Connor knew he was out of his depth. It came to him that he must try and find Harry, for the old woman's grandson had a right to read this stuff. But that was going to be easier said than done, as Nan would have said.

Hadn't Harry said he was off to Syria with his NGO? Other than being on the news a lot, Connor hadn't a clue where Syria was. It was a piece of a jigsaw of countries at the opposite end of the Mediterranean to Benidorm, a place where people were starving and blowing each other to bits. And what on earth was an NGO?

He looked up NGO on his smartphone: Non-Governmental Organisation. There were a couple of examples – the Red Cross and Save the Children. Connor had heard of both of those. Hadn't the old biddy mentioned that Harry was going off on some medical mission in Turkey? Perhaps he was a doctor.

Well, that was a start. Connor felt a rare sense of confidence in himself. Maybe he should confide in Dave and ask his advice. They got on well and trusted one another.

***

It is the most glorious day. There is to be a coffee morning in the village hall to raise money for its upkeep; if there is any surplus money, it will go the local air ambulance. The organisers will be pleased it's a fine day because the trestle tables can be outside and that may attract the odd walker or cyclist.

It is the same stalwart people time after time who keep our

little community going. Crispin and Amanda are turning out to be tremendous assets; although used to more sophisticated forms of fund-raising, they are adapting well to our usual format – coffee, tea, home-made scones and cakes, a raffle, a gossip and a good crack.

The request for raffle prizes is a convenient place to get rid of surplus birthday and Christmas presents, some recognisable from two years ago: cheap bottles of red and white wine, boxes of chocolates with the sell-by date scrubbed out, packets of notelets, a bar of soap, talcum powder. Today someone gave a pack of four toilet rolls and some fresh vegetables and seedlings, and a colouring book with crayons just in case there are grandchildren present.

I noticed that Crispin has abandoned his suede shoes and was wearing Wellies. The smart blazer with the brass buttons has disappeared and he has bought himself a Barbour.

There was a good turnout. Hoping to win the loo rolls, I bought ten pounds worth of raffle tickets. Halfway through the morning, a contingent from the old rectory appeared wearing their LGBT T-shirts. I have never felt the urge to advertise my proclivities and also I find abbreviations difficult to interpret. I am still confused by those acronyms of the Second World War, like LDV, ARP, WRNS, ATS and FANYS, ENSA, NAAFI. A few of them had caused misunderstanding, and in some cases merriment. There was ACG: two bodies had claimed this as their own, the Assistant Chaplin General and the Aerodrome Construction Group. Then there was BESA – the British Engineering Standards Association and the Bengal Entertainment Service Association.

Although I am fortunate enough to own some ISAs, I am unsure what they stand for. I have been assured that they are tax free so that must be a good thing, but only if you have not been brought up to believe that you should be contributing to society.

The LGBT contribution to the raffle prizes was four packets of vegan dehydrated shepherd's pie, which could be brought to life by the addition of boiling water, or so it said on the packet. I am going to have to learn to bite my tongue but, there again, why should I?

Mrs Parks was on her familiar round, doing refills with her giant metal teapot. Her family are fifth-generation hill-sheep farmers. She whispered in my ear, intending to be heard, 'That lot are like fish out of water. What I can't stand is their bloody self-righteousness.'

'I know, dear,' I said biting my tongue. Then I turned to the newcomers and said, 'Lovely to see new faces. Find yourselves a seat and we will be with you in a tick. I am uncertain why I used the word 'tick'. It must have been word association: shepherd's pie equals sheep, and ticks are nasty things that live in the bracken on the enclosed fell land and cause louping disease in sheep. I hear it is on the up and up in humans due to the increased number of ramblers with bare legs.

I took my cup of overly weak tea and joined them. It was all very jolly hockey sticks, as if I were back at boarding school again. I was tempted to give them one of those Keep Britain Farming stickers, which I keep in my bag to jog the memories of urban friends to remind them whence their food cometh, but I decided not to.

Instead I sat there listening. It appears their laudable efforts at growing their own vegetables have been a bit of a disaster. All the planted-out lettuce seedlings were eaten by rabbits, along with the broccoli and cabbages.

I entered into conversation with what I thought was a sensible suggestion. 'I'll ask one of my grandsons to pop over either early morning or late at night to shoot them when they're out feeding.' Forgetting that I was fraternising with vegans, I added, 'He will skin them for you and you'll have a free meal.'

It was as though I were an alien.

'Oh that's horrible! That's cruel! We'll report you to the police and the RSPCA.'

I realised that now we have a PM with a bunny-hugging wife this was becoming political. I ignored their comment and asked them how they would deal with the problem, but of course they hadn't clue.

Mrs Parks was on her rounds again with the teapot and I caught her eye, which gave me courage. I tried not to raise my voice, remembering that Fiona, my lovely Scottish cardiologist, has told me to take things easy and not to become worked up, but it is difficult when you are witnessing your way of life being destroyed by ignorance.

'The problem is that the animal-rights brigade have killed off all the humanitarian methods of pest control. I have a friend with a couple of ferrets who would help,' I said.

Their leader asked, 'How does that work?'

And back I went for one glorious day of childhood ferreting with my brothers. An early start, David with his ferret box over his shoulder – only David was allowed to handle the ferrets. He bred them and they knew him. I once tried to stroke one and it bit me.

We looked for the inhabited burrows marked by newly-dug soil and fresh droppings. Jack and I were in charge of the nets, spreading them carefully over the holes and making sure that the stake holding them was secure. Once the ferret was in the hole, the rabbits raced out at full speed like bullets from a gun, Jack running over to give the knockout blow. My job was to watch the bolt holes to make sure the ferrets didn't escape and cause havoc amongst neighbours' poultry. I still relive the excitement.

We carried the warm, flea-ridden rabbits back into the house to be dealt with in the kitchen. During the war we lived on rabbit. I remember my brothers used to keep their pelts and dry them out, then make pocket money selling them to this man who came round. He sold them on to furriers. Now this is forbidden and they go in the dustbin; you are not allowed to use fur to keep yourself warm, it has to be plastic. The furriers had bricks thrown through their windows and went out of business.

The LGBTs were looking at me with disbelief. Of course, they have never experienced real nature; they live in the world of Disneyland and TV wildlife programmes.

'Do you want a top up, Julia?' Mrs Parks was poised with her teapot and I was brought back down to earth and grateful for her intervention,

Crispin announced they were going to draw the raffle.

I didn't win the loo rolls.

***

Gloria heard Connor's laughter and was pleased to know he was happy. She called up, 'What's making you laugh?'

'Nothing.'

He just might tell Dave in the morning. He wouldn't need to mention his old biddy.

As he read on, she became sad again.

***

There are times when I almost wish I had dementia, then I would have an excuse. I would be allowed to forget all the wrong turns I have taken in my life. It is those of us who have overactive minds, that bring to the surface those instructions given when the mind is pliable and at its most receptive, who have the problems. When 'do as you would be done by' and 'think of others before yourself' become confused with 'have faith in yourself'. And I have yet to discover 'the peace of God which passeth all understanding' – I was so certain that at the end it would be there. I want my mind to leave me alone.

My thoughts are repeating themselves over and over again. If I had kept a diary this would not happen, but of course I didn't. Now all I can remember are the six or seven decades of marriage to Hugh. I wake up each morning with the smell of him.

I cannot remember him loving me other than physically, those acts of love he made so pleasurable that I forgave him the rest. Of course, I now understand why he was like that and wish I had been more understanding. The children try to reassure me. They see my distress and counter it with, 'You know, Mum darling, what a difficult person he was. Everyone found him so. When we were children we tried to get close to him, but he always put up barriers against real love.'

There was proof of all this in the carefully filed letters I found later.

The rooms are still full of him; the hoardings of Hugh's life have spilled out into every corner of the house. I spent the morning in the forbidden territory of his study, looking for a file. As I reached down to open a drawer in his old mahogany kneehole desk, his ghost passed over me and I felt a restraining hand on my wrist. He wasn't into sharing; sharing would have destroyed him as a person. He was generous with money, but not with himself.

The grandchildren are showing interest. They are leaving their smartphones unanswered and holding in their hands the painstaking letters of concern and complaint that became his hallmark. They, like me, are seeing Hugh for the first time, for he would never share his knowledge when he was alive. He did mellow a little towards the end, particularly with Harry with whom he half-connected. On occasions, Harry was allowed into his inner sanctum; it may be that Hugh saw a free spirit in Harry, something he knew he would never be. Poor old Hugh; his name and complaint were synonymous.

***

On seeing Harry's name again, Connor took it as a sign. Tomorrow he would begin his search. He would start with Save the Children because they had a charity shop in town. And he would have to look up the meaning of synonymous.

***

I left the young to it and went into the kitchen. I poured myself a large whisky and I looked out of the window hoping to see God, but He wasn't there.

I had tried hard that morning not to have a whisky before making my scrambled egg, but the two eldest grandchildren arrived unannounced and then I started worrying about what to give them for lunch. I thought there were a couple of tins of baked beans in the larder – should I offer them a beer? Better not if they were driving.

They wandered into the kitchen carrying files from Hugh's cabinet.

'Don't suppose you've got a couple of beers, Gran.'

'Yes, I think you'll find some in the dairy.' Now I shall worry myself silly until they text to say they are safely home.

'Gran, there are letters here of Grandpa's going back over

83

half a century. They're really quite interesting. He tried to stop the A66 being driven through the Lake District National Park to facilitate the manufacture of cars in West Cumberland. He objected to the Poll Tax and more recently the Iraq war – his letters are really well argued. May we take them, Gran? They might help with our dissertations. Oh, and there's a file here about a place in Australia called Fairbridge, and lots of letters from someone called John Lane. Should we keep them or chuck them out?'

'Goodness, John Lane!' I said, astonished. 'A wonderful man and I had almost forgotten him. He was a great friend of your grandfather. Don't throw them out, pop them in the sitting room and I'll look through them later. I'll just get you boys something to eat.'

'We're not boys, Granny, we are men.'

'How right you are. I keep forgetting.'

Which reminds me, I really should stop driving on the A66. It doesn't like me and the feeling is reciprocal; it scares the living daylights out of me. This grey macadam river running through the beautiful valley of Eden has become a race track for those who don't know where they are going, fed by its tributaries of minor roads, country lanes and farm tracks.

The enlightened twenty-first century has, in all aspects, returned to the twelfth. Slaughter and mayhem rule again, not contained in small pockets of violence as once they were, but digitally enhanced and spread by technology. The lilies of the field have been replaced by plastic that cannot wither and die.

Am I thinking these thoughts because whisky has clouded my judgement? Hugh would have said so; whenever I tried to enter a conversation, even with others present, he would say in that put-down way he did so well, 'Must be the whisky talking.'

My father would have said, 'You've gone as daft as a yat off its creuk,' and replenished my glass.

Now that Hugh is gone, I am allowed to make friends with people who are kind. I feel that they love me and they are such a lovely bunch. I am no longer forced to make friends with all those 'right' people who turned out to be all the wrong ones. My defences have been breached by Covid 19 and the kindness of strangers who sit around the kitchen table for a chat.

***

It came to Connor in a blinding flash: Miss would know how to find Harry. She was good at puzzles and that kind of thing. He remembered her saying that he could call on her at any time. But how could he contact her? He didn't have her mobile number and he knew that the school would not give it to him because of data protection.

He would have to write a letter addressed to her at the school. He had never written a letter in his life. Nan used to write them and say that if you wanted a reply it was good manners to enclose a stamped addressed envelope.

He found a scrap of lined paper and made a start.

My name is Connor and once I was in your class. I am the boy with red hair who sat at the back of the room next to Seb. You won't remember me.

I know this sounds silly but I am trying to find someone called Harry who I think is a doctor and I think lives in Syria and works for something called an NGO. How can I find him?

I have got a job at the recycling plant and my boss is called Dave, he's a nice bloke.

Gloria was curious when Connor asked if she had two envelopes and two stamps. She never wrote letters but sent expensive cards to people instead. On his way to work the

85

following morning he posted the letter with a feeling of excitement

Within a week there lay an envelope on the mat by the front door with his writing on it. He opened it expecting rejection and read:

Of course I remember you, Connor dear. You were always most polite.

Connor remembered the time when he had gone to her rescue, wiping the word 'dike' from the blackboard before she saw it.

I will try and help you find this person but first you must tell me why you need to find him. We live in an age of data protection and it may not be easy.

I am pleased you have found a job, and a very worthwhile one. Dave sounds a nice person.

Do you remember telling me how your grandfather worked in the sewers of London but asked me not to tell anyone because you might get teased about it. I have just come back from a holiday in the Slovak Republic, which used to be part of Czechoslovakia. In Bratislava there is a monument to a sewer worker, a figure in bronze clambering out of a manhole on a city street and resting his head on his arms. When I saw it, I thought of your great-grandfather.

I so enjoyed receiving your letter.

***

I managed to stand upright to do the Morrison's run, though had to ask for a chair at checkout and was kindly brought a glass of water. I could see the faces of those in the queue held up by my old age; two were sympathetic but the cold stare of another reminded me that I have outlived my sell-by date and am rapidly becoming an inconvenience.

The young are kind but only see what is in front of them. They cannot imagine that I was once young, just as they cannot imagine themselves becoming old.

I have never been certain of anything, certainly not the decisions I make, so trips to Morrison's have become a challenge as the choices increase. I hesitate over everything, hovering between Lurpak and Flora, salted and unsalted, until nice Nina spots me and comes over with, 'We meet again. How are you? Can I help you?'

An elbow nearly knocked the stick from my hand. Today Nina was on checkout number nine. She is lovely and she looks out for me. She caught my eye and gave me a reassuring smile. I think she is an asylum seeker and I know she speaks three languages.

When I got home I realised I had picked up a pack of lamb chops instead of the intended pork chops and became quite upset for I had planned carefully, had some apple sauce and sage-and-onion stuffing at the ready, but no mint sauce or redcurrant jelly. I felt uneasy for the whole weekend. How could a trivial error create such a mood swing when half the world is starving?

***

Connor knew there was a proper word to describe his thoughts. Miss had used a word when things became important – 'imperative' – and it was now imperative that he found Harry and told him about the stuff his grandmother had written. He had become this old biddy's guardian angel.

It was going to be difficult explaining about her in a letter; he would have to write again to Miss, perhaps ask for her mobile number and whether he could meet her to explain things. He knew both these options would meet with resistance; he understood that communication with teachers outside school was frowned upon. It could lead to all sorts of misunderstandings – you only had to look at the Sunday newspapers to read about teachers having it off with younger pupils, imaginary or otherwise. He didn't want to put Miss in a difficult position, and he wasn't sure if she was right about data protection when you were allowed to say really nasty things about people on Twitter and Facebook and no one stopped you.

It took Connor a week to write a second letter asking if he could phone her or perhaps come and see her. He didn't know how to write down what was going on in his mind, but it had become imperative.

The word *imperative* must have done it, for a fortnight later one of the cheap brown envelopes he had bought at the supermarket was pushed through the letterbox. He just had time to read it before leaving for work.

Dear Connor

I sense something is worrying you. Here is my mobile number – phone me and we can arrange to meet somewhere.

***

I got home safely, though well aware that I should not be driving, at least not until I have my cataracts done. The helm wind was in its element, so strong that I couldn't open the car door against it. Its roar could be heard from the top of Cross Fell.

I never mind the elements controlling me – being in their hands is far more reliable than depending on humans – so I sat in the car waiting for the wind to subside, catch its breath for a moment. When it did, I made a dash for it, my latch key at the ready.

I have never been afraid of death for I am blessed with belief, but I am afraid for the remainder of my life. I also fear what my death will leave behind, the confusion to be sorted out and binned by other people, all that gubbins which I once thought important.

The youngsters are insisting that they buy me a commode for my bedside and they won't take no for an answer. I have texted them all to say I do not want a commode. I just want someone to help me with my income tax, which I am trying to self-assess, and help me use the computer to send a short story I have written, which I thought the *Oldie* magazine might find of interest. I just need to test the waters, to see if freedom of speech is still alive in this sceptred isle. From where I am standing, it doesn't appear to be. Wokes are in command, re-writing history with their clever, clever self-absorption.

I know I haven't a hope in hell of being published at my age but I still have something to say, even if those younger than me find it embarrassing and don't want to listen. I need to succeed on my own terms, live at last by my own rules. Go recognised.

I wonder how this generation will be judged a century from now when biometrics control everything including the soul, and technical recognition is the norm. Obviously I dare not mention this to anyone; if I do, they will consider me gaga. Not that you are allowed to use the word 'gaga' because the cool word is 'dementia'.

Little incidents are short-circuiting my brain, and my memory is playing havoc with my peace of mind. It's this guilt thing again. I am now on beta blockers to stop this happening. The lovely Scottish cardiologist found a bed for me in the local hospital right in the middle of the pandemic. We had quite a chat and ended up discussing religious hatred. I reminded her that in my day there had been blasphemy laws which stopped people making a mockery of the beliefs of others, but these were repealed in 1968 by some leftie human-rights fanatics quoting freedom of speech. Since then, hatred has taken off.

'You may have a point,' she said, and I knew she was thinking about it.

To live in this beautiful, isolated place is one of the privileges I am fortunate to have been given. I caught God's eyes again this morning; they had a sad look, worn out and weeping as He witnessed the prostitution of his planet. Do the fingers of His son's pierced hands feel any throb of goodness as daily He measures the pulse of mankind?

I must make a decision soon. Although the A66 was quieter yesterday and I feel safer behind the wheel of a car than I do walking downstairs, the time has come to think about giving up driving.

Once upon a time, in that never-never land of youth, my body raced up and down the stairs three at a time, jumping from top to bottom in one go, egged on by the exuberance of youth and my brothers for a bet. Now I dare not venture upstairs or down without a banister or grab rail, a door handle or a walking stick, and that cumbersome thing around my neck on which a button reads SOS. It will bring kindly neighbours running to my door if I fall, probably muttering, 'It's batty old Julia again. Too many whiskies, I suspect.'

My body has shrunk, but my bones appear larger; they stick out and hit things, they get tired easily and can be painful at times. I get tired easily. On occasion I have to sit down halfway up the stairs and catch my breath. Then I remember Mother's voice,

> 'Halfway up the stairs is the stair where I sit.
> There isn't any other stair quite like it.

It isn't at the bottom and it isn't at the top,
But that is the stair where I always stop.'
Recently I heard her voice again:
'Yesterday upon the stair,
I met a man who wasn't there.
He wasn't there again today,
I do so wish…'

That reminds me: I must try and dissuade the children from wasting their time investigating stairlifts.

I have been watching the Olympics, trying to keep up to date. I've been told it is patriotic to do so – 'Haven't you got some national pride?' they say. I try to explain that it has all dried up, and those bronzed, muscled, nubile bodies are foreign to me now.

The flame of truth being passed from one generation to the next – it just doesn't happen that way. New generations have their own agenda, and this freedom of speech versus hate crime is becoming a bit of a thing. I wish I was too young to remember the Hitler Youth then I wouldn't get so worked up, but unfortunately I do. A generation of German *kinder* taught to betray their parents, spy on them if they suspected that they may be out of step with the goosesteps of those in power. Isn't our dear old country in danger of doing just that? I don't want to believe it; I would prefer to believe that I am going mad.

***

Connor read the words, not certain what they all meant and what she was getting at. His nan used to go on in the same jumbled up sort of way. He had sort of understood her, but when it was written down it was more difficult to understand, a bit like trying to have a conversation with someone on Zoom. The background caught your eye and you became more interested in the wallpaper.

It had been a foul day at the plant, pouring with rain and lots of people putting things in the wrong places. He would try and get off work early, buy a Big Mac on the way home, have a quick wash and then phone Miss.

Later that night he sat on the bed, daring himself to dial. It was like putting his hand up in class, but this time there was no Seb to distract him. He almost chickened out, but then he heard her voice. 'Hello?'

'Hello, Miss. It's me, Connor.'

'Oh Connor, how lovely! It's so good to hear from you.'

Connor was unsure how to answer so there was a bit of a pause, then she said, 'Might I suggest, Connor, that we meet up one evening. Perhaps you could come straight from work. What about the pizza parlour in Botchergate? Do you know it?'

Connor had a quick think. Yes, he did know it and there was a bike stand outside.

'What day would suit you? I can manage tomorrow about 5.30.'

'That's fine, Miss. I'll be there.' He decided he would wear his fluorescent jacket with his name on it. It would make Miss think more of him, think he was making something of his life.

CHAPTER 8

I am having a really good day today. I am bursting with positivity and haven't even had my 10.30 am whisky yet. My firstborn is with me.

I forget that she is in her seventies; how time flies. She has made the long drive north from Cambridge to see me, ventured north to the city of her birth. I hope it is because of love and not duty. We don't always see eye to eye, and usually end up having the odd spat. We are poles apart politically but very close in all the things that matter. Of course, it's that generation thing again.

She is now a leading academic, and her opinion is sought by the media. She appears on TV whenever a professor is required to fill a gap. I remember when she was four, her aunt gave her a doll and she christened it Palestrina. Even at that age she was streets ahead of me in the intellectual stakes.

***

Miss was there when Connor arrived, warming her hands on a mug of coffee. She put it down and stood up, then came towards him with outstretched arms and gave him a hug. He felt himself blushing. She looked prettier, younger than she did in the classroom.

'So good to see you again, Connor. You're looking well. I

like the jacket. You must be hungry – order yourself a pizza. It's on me.'

They sat down. Connor removed the fluorescent jacket and hung it on the back of his chair with his name showing. It was an awkward thing to sit down in because it crumpled up and engulfed him.

When his pizza arrived, Miss said, 'Now, what is this all about, Connor?'

'Well it's this old woman, Miss. I think her name's Julia…' He tried to explain as best he could, telling a few white lies along the way about how he had come by the hard drive. He told her he'd found all this stuff on it and how there was this bloke called Harry who was Julia's grandson. Connor said he'd met him and this coloured girl at the recycling place and somehow the old woman's writing had taken over his life.

'I haven't finished reading it all yet. It's a bit muddled, sort of like a diary but in the wrong order. She talks about things a bit like my Nan did.'

'I can see that you feel passionate about this, Connor, and I'll do what I can to help. Is it that you want to find Harry to give him the hard drive?'

He didn't answer because he was unsure what he wanted.

Miss continued. 'I think our best plan is for you to finish reading it all then put it on a memory stick. In the meantime, I'll have a think about the best way to go about finding Harry. You say you think he's a doctor – you may be right. Perhaps his partner with the child is also a doctor – and you say she was Asian? That will shorten the odds a bit. If all you've learned is accurate, they'll now have a son of about eight and a baby about one years old. I'll make some enquiries locally – there may be people who know who Julia is. If Harry is abroad, we shall have to widen our horizons.'

***

I can't say that going in an ambulance was on my bucket list but I've achieved it. Had one of my blackouts shortly after Sarah returned to Cambridge, hit my head and was found by my dear neighbours. I was apparently rambling a bit whilst I was strapped down on the stretcher, then I came round to find this delicious young man stroking my hand. The ambulance journey would have been top of the bucket list had I known that he was waiting for me.

His name was Brian and we chatted. He had been a paramedic for three years and was younger than my grandchildren. 'We'd better take your slippers off,' he said, and removed the old Marks and Sparks moccasins which had taken me around South Africa fifteen years previously.

'Look after those slippers, they are important to me,' I said. 'They once stood on hallowed ground. How on earth could a human being emerge from that concrete cage after eighteen years without rancour or malice?'

Brian thought I was having another turn, but I remember being fully conscious.

'I spent a day on Robben Island and spoke to one of his guards, who was now acting as a guide. He told me that during his incarceration the thing Mandela missed most was not his freedom but the sound of children's voices at play. I stood in that cell for less than eighteen minutes. Those slippers have felt oppression.'

'We're almost there. They'll sort you out,' Brian said.

I am home again, living on a diet of beta blockers.

I have tried to explain faith to my children and grandchildren but am unsure whether I have got through to them, I sometimes think they tell me they understand just to set my mind at rest.

95

When you have lived out your life and are waiting for the end, the last thing you need is the knowledge that you have got the whole of it bloody wrong. Being told you have by others is almost impossible to take on board. The sword of Damocles hangs over your head and the time is running out to make a change.

Poured myself a large whisky and switched on Bob Dylan. Hi, Mr Tambourine Man. He's telling me to forget about today until tomorrow.

Tomorrow would have been our eightieth – eighty-first? – wedding anniversary. The weather forecast promises a crisp autumn day, as it was on our wedding day. Not a cloud in a bright blue sky, the earth crisp and frosted by an early November cold snap. The words of the marriage service fresh in our ears, Hugh concerned that I might catch cold as the outside photos were being taken. Concern withered and died; only duty remained.

And it was with that sense that I decided to try and walk up to the top land to his grave and have a final talk with him. Physically it would be a challenge, but I had two walking sticks, my right knee was wearing its brace, the emergency button was on my wrist and my mobile was fully charged. I should perhaps have warned the neighbours where I was going, but they would only have tried to dissuade me

I tried to imagine what was left of Hugh: a heap of bones picked clean by worms and the myriad insects that live in that underworld. Perhaps moles, too, for they are not averse to carrion. Maybe they are getting even after all those years of persecution.

Hugh's skull intact, the stronghold of his thoughts of unforgiveness. That was his philosophy and it made him so unhappy; it resurfaced after his death with the boxes of letters I found in his study.

I found one the other day, its envelope stating that it was from Buckingham Palace, with ER in the bottom left-hand corner. It addressed him as Esquire and was dated 28.05.98. He had never mentioned to me that he was in correspondence with the palace.

Hugh had written protesting about the forthcoming state visit of the Emperor of Japan and the decision to confer on him the Order of the Garter. It saddened me that, after fifty years, he still bore a grudge. He went to his death still bearing it.

The Queen's reasoned response, relayed through a senior correspondence officer, said it all: *It is a recognition of today's friendship between our nations and in no way detracts from the debt which is owed to all who fought and suffered in the Far East during the last war.*

I can hear Hugh's voice from the grave dismissing this.

The last time I walked up to the high land to pay my respects was in springtime. The patch where he is buried was a mass of bright-blue forget-me-nots which had self-seeded; carried by the southerly wind, they had found there resting place in the disturbed earth of Hugh's internment. They were a splash of colour to remind me that there had been good times. The wind always knows what it's doing. Bob Dylan and I both understand that if you trust the elements you don't need to watch the weather forecast.

I would have liked to say a little prayer but I knew how much Hugh disliked anything religious, so I hummed Bob Dylan, the words in my head. I apologised for not being the babe that Hugh was looking for all those years ago.

I remembered an earlier visit to his grave in deep midwinter when snow lay on the ground and I nearly joined him, nearly died of exposure before I was rescued by some trespassing skiers…

It took an hour for my old body to drag itself up the lane and across the enclosed fell land, though less time to make the descent. And tomorrow lay ahead with the promise of a good day, for I had a dentist's appointment to look forward to.

A life's span has metamorphosed dentists, and my childhood terror is fading. But I still remember the overwhelming smell of gas that seeped into the street before the door opened and you were ushered in to the dark underworld which faced north. I remember being lifted into that vast black leather chair, fighting against the heavy rubber thing placed over my face, the hissing of gas as it filled my lungs until they were on the point of bursting. I remember waking up and being violently sick, and Mr Morton – who looked like Neville Chamberlain with his high starched collar and unsmiling ferret face – hanging over me.

Now it is lovely Mr Patel and hopefully tomorrow, in between the drilling, we shall discuss the partition of India. The soothing sounds of the sitar in the background make analgesic hardly necessary.

I could do with some sitar music right now. The wokes are at it again, destroying the memories of honourable men, writing stuff for their own self-seeking aggrandisement. In a different age their words would have been deemed libellous.

They are having a go at Kingsley Fairbridge, that great philanthropist who founded a farm school in Australia's outback a century ago to teach orphan children a trade and self-reliance. This time I have proof of liberal duplicity because I have the file the boys found in Hugh's study with letters and testimonies by those sent there in the 1930s to start a new life. They were given opportunities that would have been out of reach in Dr Barnardo's.

Kingsley Fairbridge was the father I never had...

I am so grateful for what he did for us as kids ... he is one of the great unsung heroes...

I have tried to model my life on his unselfish work...

One boy in particular, John Lane, went on to become a writer and musician because of the Fairbridge scheme. Hugh met him because of the war: he was one of the thousands of Australian POWs captured by the Japanese and repatriated by the British Navy. During that sea voyage to his homeland, he and Hugh became friends. John and his wife stayed with us whenever they were in the UK.

Sadly he died of motor neurone disease. He last spoke to Hugh on the phone in 2005, Hugh had sent a donation for an avenue of trees being planted at Fairbridge. In the file there is a photo of John standing beside Hugh's tree.

I fear there may be a balaclava-clad activists hiding around the corner wielding chainsaws.

Illiberalists have taken hold; they are a vociferous bunch, seeing offence in everything, shouting abuse. Politicians jump on the bandwagon when they should know better, asking just about everyone when they should say sorry to everyone else.

Have just looked up the word 'liberal' in my Hamlyn's dictionary: *favourable to or in accord with the policy of leaving the individual as unrestricted as possible in opportunities for self-expression or self-fulfilment.*

Therein lies the problem to the detriment of the truth, and I'm beginning to get worked up about it.

Had a whisky far too early in the day and found the phone number of the Liberal Party on Google. I also found a receipt in the Fairbridge file for a cheque Hugh had sent many years ago. I said a quick thank you to him for his immaculate filing system and said sorry for not really understanding him. No wonder he got so cross with me.

CHAPTER 9

Mr Patel didn't let me down. Obviously there was that elephant in the room, the misconceptions about colonialism that are now in vogue, when everything good about India is belittled by those who never experienced it. We have entered the grey zone of half-truths and mistrust.

Although he calls me Julia, I don't know Mr Patel's Christian name. I am too polite to ask, and of course it will not be a Christian name but a Hindu or Muslim one.

***

Connor was not familiar with dentists. When one had been necessary, his real mother never bothered; if he got toothache, he was sent to school as usual and a teacher was left to deal with it. He couldn't understand why the old biddy spent so much time writing about her dentist. Nan had false teeth, which she took out to eat and put in on Sundays when relatives came to visit.

***

It was quite an obstacle race to establish Mr Patel's origins. I realised that if I asked him straight 'Where do you come from?' it might appear racist, so I enquired at reception and the girl said Manchester. When I persevered with a 'before that', she said Birmingham.

I decided to face the situation head on and, during my third appointment, asked Mr Patel, 'Were your forebears from India?'

'Yes.'

'Which part?' You never know, there might have been some slight connection with Hugh's father's colonial past, and I have always believed in fate.

'Ahmednagar.'

I asked him to repeat it, for I thought I had misheard and the coincidence was too great.

'Ahmednagar. My father was at the medical school there,' he said.

'That's where my husband's father was initially stationed in the thirties, before being seconded to Number 6 party of the Indian Army in Bangalore to help with the survey of that vast country.' He was one of a team of mapmakers of the unchartered wild areas of northern India. Hugh had told me that there is a church pew somewhere in Kashmir on which his father's name is engraved in appreciation of his work. In 1944 he was badly wounded whilst preventing the Japanese from invading India from Burma. He held the Burma Star.

I managed to convey this between the drillings, and Mr Patel replied, 'The evil men do lives after them – the good is oft interred with their bones.' He was quoting Shakespeare, and it sealed an understanding. A special kind of friendship was established.

It was two appointments later that we got onto the subject of the partition of India.

How desperate mankind has become. We have inadvertently torn up the guidelines for happiness, but they are still out there for the taking, waiting to be stuck together again by those with the energy to try.

I leave my computer on all the time so that it is ready to welcome my thoughts when something occurs to me, hold them for me, give me a chance to think things out and delete when necessary. It is much more fun than keeping a diary, for memory isn't chronological; it jumps up at you from time to time when you are least expecting it.

***

Connor thought that was just like when he got a hard on. The stuff about India was quite interesting. He couldn't imagine a world before the Internet, when people had to find things out for themselves. He had never been anywhere wild, he hadn't even been properly abroad. When he was six or seven, his real mother had taken him to Benidorm. He had expected wilderness but it was just like going to Blackpool, except it was warmer. There weren't even any donkeys to ride, and his fair skin didn't like the hot sun. He had been disappointed.

***

Funerals are coming at me thick and fast. I have been to three this month and paid my last respects to two people I never respected in life, wondering why the hell I was there. I listened to the vicar making an effort, trying to say nice things about someone she knew only too well.

Am I now top of the heap? Is it my turn next? I had better acquaint myself with the procedure.

Independent living is a bit of a myth because it isn't independent at all. I am totally reliant on walking sticks and a trolley thing with wheels, and I have given in. Instead of a lover at my bedside, I have a commode. Its companion, my faithful Zimmer frame, is strategically placed so that when I have to

102

get out of bed for a pee, which is often, I have *something* not *someone* reliable to hang onto.

It is important that I keep my motivation and don't let myself drift into reliance on others. Today I made some meringues. The hens in the village have gone into overdrive and their surplus eggs were left on the doorstep by kind neighbours. Am really pleased with myself!! It is nearing Christmas again, and they can be my contribution to the festivities; I am not expected to contribute any more but it is a pleasant feeling when I do. I have my dear old Aga, which has been my companion for almost sixty years. Its slow oven makes the production of meringues the easiest thing in the world. It takes things slowly for the best results; poor confused mankind is in too much of a hurry.

***

My Nan used to say that, thought Connor

***

I looked up and saw a snowflake. Five minutes earlier, the sun had been shining with that winter intensity. The snowflake was on its own, larger than they usually are. It hesitated for a moment, unsure which way the wind would take it. It hovered until it was caught by a southerly and then went north. Others came to join it.

I'm listening to Bob Dylan at full blast. The young postie – he looks about twelve – delivering mail to Crispin and Amanda heard it. Although he hadn't anything for me, he knocked on the door and smilingly asked, 'Bob Dylan?' He is called Alexander and told me he is saving up to go to Peru. Because I thought what a splendid ambition that was, on the spur of the moment I gave him a tenner. It was one of those lame-dog episodes that so annoyed Hugh, but now I can do it without censure.

I am aware that I have been neglecting my feet. I should have phoned the nice Polish podiatrist who put up a sign in the village to come and have a look at them, reassure me that my big toenails are not ingrowing, even though my mind is. The nasty smell, of which I am aware when I take off my tights, is coming from a small area between my right-hand little toe and its neighbouring digit.

I am over the moon because I got up early, did my feet and managed to cut my toenails without falling over or passing out when I bent down. I am bloody well not giving up yet.

I was encouraged when I drove into town yesterday for an appointment with my solicitor – she isn't really my solicitor but one of a group of pretty young girls who have replaced the old male family friend of my youth.

It is Mothering Sunday again, that spiritual time when faith and nature congratulate mothers for doing a good job and they, in their turn, thank God for helping them through it. Somehow it has been taken out of the mouths of refugees giving birth in a tent and put into the hands of the card-producing industry. The voice once spread the word; now it is technology spreading the imagined word of God. Or perhaps I have had too many whiskies.

Thanks to Morrison's continuing to deliver to me at home, I have a good supply of Famous Grouse. I have got to know Stella well; she is a delightful person who cheers me up no end. We discovered we have mutual acquaintances. She lets me know whenever the Grouse is on offer. Although I felt a bit guilty about panic buying and hoarding, to know it is there is wonderfully reassuring, the same way I feel about Bob Dylan, my computer and the plumber.

***

Connor suddenly felt immeasurably sad. First she'd been talking about Christmas and meringues, and now it was Mothering Sunday. He realised that the posts on the computer had been made at longer intervals, that his old biddy was slowing down.

CHAPTER 10

What on earth do they mean by gender fluency? Who are *they*? For what purpose are they engendering doubt in the underdeveloped minds of poor little blighters already struggling with GCSEs and having to decide between muesli and Cocopops? I think it's called illiberal liberalism, or is it illogical liberalism? I am unsure and will have to ask Sarah next time she comes north.

My family were once passionate Liberals, and before that Whigs.

For Whigs now read wokes. All this ghastly finger pointing, this awful blame game now being played out – it is the new national pastime. The words 'misadventure' and reason have been bowdlerised from a nation's vocabulary. The new generation game is 'Your Generation Got Nothing Right'; throw the dice and get a double, find some skeleton in an elder statesman's cupboard and destroy him. Pass go, get out of prison and win the game.

There are skeletons in every family, and I suppose mine has its fair share of good and bad. I am well-acquainted with James, the good great-uncle on mother's side, who died before I was born. He studied medicine in Edinburgh at the end of the nineteenth century and was a friend and colleague of Joseph Lister. They worked together in Paris on pioneering research into antiseptics. Afterwards James returned to his Cumbrian birthplace to found a medical practice and fight to have a sewerage system built in the town. The practice still going strong after a hundred and twenty years. It was where I was given my Covid jabs. The local newspaper tells me the sewer may be in need of repair.

I am grateful to the county archivist in Carlisle for keeping all the family papers safe, otherwise they would be engulfed by the clutter and chaos in which I feel I now live. I must remember to tell Harry where they are – he may not know that they exist. We text occasionally but I hesitate to burden him further for he is facing Armageddon in the Middle East and this all seems so trivial.

***

Connor thought it interesting that even posh people were interested in sewers.

***

Of course there were family bad apples who did very well for themselves. It is purported that one sixteenth-century adventurer, an earlier James from a branch of Mother's family, followed in the footsteps of Dick Whittington and took himself off to London to seek his fortune. He trained as a lawyer and became a judge, married Elizabeth, a daughter of the Lord Mayor of London, and never looked back. In order to curry favour with the King (I think it was James 1), who had a paranoid fear of witches, this forbear did a lot of finger pointing. He was famous for denouncing poor, simple, country folk as witches, particularly in the Pendle area, and making certain they were hanged.

For this service he was given a knighthood and ended

up as Judge Sir James. My mother still bore his surname four centuries later, before she married my father. Certain things never change, but the meaning of words do.

As a child, when I encountered an unfamiliar word, Mother would say, 'Go and look it up.' The dictionaries in our home were read as often as the *Beano* and the *Dandy*, scuffed, their backs broken through overuse. We believed what we read in our dictionaries.

I remember hearing the word 'sodomite' as I sat next to my father in church. I always went with him to matins, where he acted as a sidesman and took the collection, which somehow made me feel important. 'Sod-o-mite' sounded like a fun word; it slips off the tongue like ac-o-nite. I looked it up in *The Oxford Dictionary* and it mentioned the word 'bestiality'; I thought it must be a printing error, so I went to the *Chambers Twentieth Century Dictionary* and the definition was 'depravity'. And then my favourite, the *Hamlyn's Encyclopaedic World Dictionary*, mentioned perversion.

How did my generation and the generations before get it all so wrong? It takes courage to reach old age, to watch your values be overtaken and overturned by ones which go against the grain. You need courage to watch a Parliament that once you held in high esteem now anxious to ingratiate itself with the computer-clicking mob. It is no longer the voice of the people but the voice of something else.

I feel a little peeved that sodomy is now the in thing, and at the same time they have banned fox hunting. I have never experienced sodomy, though I suspect many of the Honourable Members may have, but I have followed the foot packs on the Lakeland Fells many times. The hounds relish their responsibility, a look of pure joy on their faces as they give tongue. The cry of the hounds, which John Peel oft times led, has been replaced by baying of packs of pink pride. But at least the hounds have retained their dignity.

The question 'D'ye Ken John Peel?' is no longer asked, for to answer in the affirmative might attract a brick through your window. Once it was the anthem of my county and it is as familiar to me as the national anthem and 'Oh God Our Help in Ages Past'. Busting your gut in the pub on Saturday evening to reach the top note of Peel's 'View Halloo' as the Border Regiment marched to its beat. It is rarely heard now, but sometimes at the small local agricultural shows it comes over the tannoy and old men weep.

I still have my dear old *Hamlyn's Encyclopaedic World Dictionary*. It is my literary bible and has survived many moves. Its red bindings have come adrift, its gold leaf is faded and its pages are as thin as tissue paper, but its interior still holds the truth. Words may have changed their meaning but the alphabet is still constant and the exquisite pen-and-ink sketches as sharp as ever; open any page and they are there, miniscule illustrations.

I opened it at L the other day, and there was a drawing of a larkspur and further down the page an intricate surgeon's drawing of the larynx. I really should try and find a bookbinder because one day it will give up on me and then what will Stephen, my academic son-in-law, say? He refers to it constantly during our annual Boxing Day battles to win at Scrabble, which he always does.

It's just as well my wrists have become too weak to lift it for, should I do so, it would surely fall to pieces on the floor. It now lives on the kitchen table where I spend most of my time trying to keep warm next to the Aga.

My faith has never really been tested, other than in going to church and paying lip service to God. I have not suffered in Belsen and come through it with my faith intact; nor have I given birth in a refugee camp or endured many of the hells mankind has inflicted upon itself. There have been family sufferings, losing uncles and cousins in WW2. And my darling brother Jack died in a car crash due to his devil-may-care attitude to life. How like Jack is Harry.

Mother coped well with that tragedy; she did not seek counselling but prayed quietly and kept herself busy spring cleaning the kitchen. Those who criticised Jack for his irresponsibility with overheard asides of 'he had it coming', were reminded that, at the age of twenty-one during the partition of India, he had offered his services as a fully-qualified pilot. He took part in the airlift of thousands of women and children from the slaughter and suffering which faced them in the never-ending exodus of the innocents when India was divided. The barbarism was created by the religious intransigence and personal and political jealousies of their leaders.

It was the first time Jack had ever flown a Dakota and I can remember him being rather chuffed with himself until he witnessed the massacre, the blood and bodies of women and children.

I have another dentist appointment next week. Whilst Mr Patel is rooting around in my mouth, I hope to get a word in to put the matter straight, for I am weary of Hugh's colonial forbears having to take the blame It was not they who caused the mayhem.

I suspect Mr Patel already knows this, for he once told me that his grandparents, newlywed with a child on the way, fled persecution in the land of their birth. All the same, I shall tell him how family anecdote has it that Jack flew a Dakota plane to Lahore almost single-handed, then stripped out the interior to make more room and ferried thousands of civilians to safety.

Could it be that Jack rescued Mr Patel's grandparents? Fate and coincidence intertwined? It is a pleasant 'maybe' to carry with you during bad times. And then I sometimes wonder if witnessing that slaughter of the innocents might have made Jack put his foot down too far on the accelerator a fortnight later.

Thinking of refugees reminds me of Harry. Before he left for the Middle East, he hugged me and said, 'You know, Granny darling, you overthink things.'

I suppose I do. Harry knows me better than most for he added, 'And consequently you over react.'

How bloody wimpish the western world has become. It has happened so quickly, within my lifetime, within my four-score years and ten.

I really must stop watching telly – nothing but abuse and we have become sex obsessed in all the wrong ways. I quickly switch to *Frasier* to retain my sanity, and have a good laugh at the grotesqueness of the act of procreation.

Which reminds me, I have just been delivered home after a most stimulating evening amongst a group of young people. They are friends of the grandchildren of dear Tom and Maureen, who were my oldest and dearest friends. Sadly they popped their clogs years ago, but to be remembered by their grandchildren was deeply moving and enormous fun.

They must have found my phone number in Maureen's old address book. Holidaying in the Lakes, they felt they should give me a buzz and ask me to join them for a bite to eat. I explained that nowadays I don't go out at night and am usually tucked up in bed by 6.30.

'Don't worry,' one of them said. 'We'll pick you up and run you home.'

In a rash moment I must have said yes. I remember

mentioning that it wouldn't just be me coming; there is this collapsible thing with wheels that I now need to hang onto when I walk.

'No worries.'

I doubled my dose of beta blockers in the morning. It has been a long while since I enjoyed myself so much; to be in stimulating company and feel young again was a joy. And it was not just a bite to eat, more Nigella Lawson, and there were other guests.

Towards the end of the meal, tongues loosened. Climate change was mentioned and led to the subject of over-population. A pretty young girl on the opposite side of the table said, 'My parents had some friends who only had sex when they wished to procreate.'

A man on my side of the table – I think his name was Piers – replied, 'My God, that's pretty noble.'

It was the word 'noble' that struck me; other than in its aristocratic sense, it is a word you hardly ever hear nowadays. After that, the crack got humorous and mildly bawdy.

Looked up the word 'noble' in my beloved Hamlyn, I read: *of an exalted moral character or excellence ... admirable in dignity.* They both seemed to fit the bill.

Sex was never mentioned when I was young but we seemed to get there in the end. Now it appears to be the be-all and end-all of life. Absolutely everything appears to revolve around it. I can remember a time when I was dangled on the knees of father's friends; they hugged and kissed me as my father did, and I always felt secure. Of course there were dirty old men in my life, as there are in every woman's, they are part of the garden of Eden. But I was fortunate because my mother had forewarned me. However scant her sex education may have been, it served its purpose well. 'Everyone is born with instinct, so trust yours,' she would say. 'If you feel uncomfortable in a situation, detach yourself from it. Don't accept sweets from strangers.' But now, because of the clever-cleverness of man, the strangers arrive unseen on line.

Living on a farm, copulation was all around me. I watched one of Father's mares reject the visiting stallion by kicking him in the teeth, so I knew what to do. Procreation has become a bit of a minefield for real men; they were brought up to be assertive, be a bit of a lad, behave as nature intended if the human race is to continue. They are in for a rocky time.

I used to agree with the feminist movement but now they have lost the plot. The fun of coquettishness is disallowed, and they have started saying foolish things like 'freezing your eggs is empowering'. My father gave me a 4.10 rifle at the age of ten and taught me how to shoot rabbits alongside my brothers. He was a true feminist; that was the gender fluency of my day.

I stayed in bed until midday and switched channels again. I watched a debate in the House of Commons; what a delight to hear the Speaker's northern accent. No nonsense and a sense of humour, a male Betty Boothroyd – I wonder if she is still alive.

***

Connor was feeling that all this was getting out of hand when his mobile rang. He could tell by the sound of her voice that Miss was excited.

'I've tracked down your Harry. It turns out he's a local lad. He went to school in the north of the county and was one of their star pupils. His parents are still alive and live in the Borders somewhere. I think we should meet up again, Connor. It's difficult to discuss things over the phone. What about the Pizza Hut on Botchergate again on Thursday evening?'

'Fine.' He liked the way Miss said 'your Harry' as though he were in charge, but he thought he would have liked the meeting to be a bit more private. Botchergate, with its bars, nightclubs and amusement arcades, was a magnet for his classmates after six o'clock. He didn't want Seb spotting him with Miss through the window, putting out his tongue and holding up a tin of lager.

He needed to get a move on, try and finish reading the whole thing. He was beginning to find all this 'taking your innards out and examining them' stuff a bit of a drag. He hoped there might be a bit more about India. The bit about the Pendle witches was interesting – he might ask Miss about them.

But the boring stuff continued.

***

Of course I am well aware that if I mention any of this to my children they will assume I am on the point of dementia and whisk me off to goodness knows where to be diagnosed by some snowflake with an honours degree in psychology.

Christianity no longer ticks the right boxes; it has become difficult to live with, like not having the right type of mattress to get a good night's sleep. Muslims appear so much more certain of their faith. They are prepared to stop what they are doing, prostrate themselves and pray, and no one turns a hair nor takes a blind bit of notice other than to turn away with an embarrassed look on their face. I cannot help feeling that if I had ever felt the urge to say the Lord's Prayer out loud in the check-out queue in Morrison's, the manager would be called, even the police.

The human race is about to destroy itself but there's not much I can do about it at my age. The beta blockers stop me from worrying, but they are little more than a temporary and flimsy fence against the hordes invading my mind.

Coronavirus still dominates the headlines, which may be a good thing. It has made people realise how deep the morass is into which we have allowed ourselves to sink. Let's pray the era of celeb worship and false Gods may be dwindling and a virus will put an end to vanity. But the four horsemen of the apocalypse are backstage, waiting for the prompter to remind them that it is time for the finale.

I really must stop thinking like this or I will go dotty. The self-isolation on dark, cold, winter evenings isn't exactly helping. I would like to say thank you to all those gallant NHS workers, but I am not into media-driven 'clap for carers' routines. The slogan has other connotations, and may be misinterpreted. Thank yous seemed more personal when I was young.

Meeting me off the train on my return for the holidays from yet another miserable term at boarding school, Father insisted that the engine driver be thanked for bringing me back safely. The excitement of being home, the joy of clambering into the old familiar bull-nosed Morris with its distinctive number plate BRM 777, smelling again the comfort of wet leather and dogs and the longing to be reunited with my surrogate sisters, Nellie the cook and Thelma the housemaid, was put on hold.

We would walk the length of the platform to the head of the train through the steam from the engine, its huge pistons at the ready, anxious to be off again. The driver, leaning out through the heat and smoke for a breather, would see my father and salute; they had been through the First World War together. The stoker in the background, also taking a break with the sweat pouring from his blackened face, would take off his cap and then replace it.

Through the hissing heat, the driver would reach down from the footplate to shake my hand. I could feel the heat on my face from the red-hot coals. The driver would cup his hand behind his ear to hear my thank you over the noise, and accept the half-crown pressed into his hot, oily hand. From thereon I knew to trust hands like that; it is the manicured ones that I mistrust.

***

Connor was unsure what a half-crown was. He knew what a halfpenny was because Nan had told him tales of them; playing truant from school, her brothers and fellow absconders used to place halfpennies on the railway lines before the express came through. It whooshed over them, flattening them and doubling their size. To own a halfpenny squashed by *The Royal Scot* or *Mallard* gained extra kudos in the school playground.
His old biddy was still yattering on.

***

During the pandemic even the Jehovah's Witnesses stopped coming. I had always credited them with tenacity; if they'd thought about it, this could have been their finest hour. They could stand on the back doorstep crowing, ' I told you so!'

I have always passed the time of day with them but I tend to cut them off in full flow with, 'I am on your side, I know where you're coming from.' I truly do, but I do not wish to become too involved, which shows all too plainly my duplicity.

I still do not know who I really am. That makes me think of Mother; I am pretty certain she understood who she was. I have carried around a false image of my mother. She was known in the family as a tough nut, a rather unforgiving person who had gone through two world wars and played her part on the home front in the Red Cross. When Father died she did not grieve, nor did she act the merry widow, whereas on Hugh's death I was pleased to be let off the leash of dutiful wife after all those years of uneasy marriage.

I have blotted out those years; sadly, at the same time I have lost my children's childhoods. I am truly seeing things face to face and not through a glass darkly. Now, because he is no longer with me, I am beginning to feel sorry for Hugh. Having never been shown love before he met me, he didn't know what it was. A kind of suspicion filled the vacuum.

It was not Hugh's fault; I was too young and we both entered willingly into matrimonial bliss in that beautiful northern Norman church on a November day. The earth was carpeted by a glittering white frost and the sky so cloudless and blue – what could possibly go wrong? Surrounded by well-wishers, I left the house on the arm of my father.

It is the small, unexpected incidents in childhood that shape and distort lives, that imprint themselves on the subconscious. Balmy days of innocence can suddenly change direction. Galloping behind Father, playing ponies as he mowed the grass on those extensive, privileged lawns of my youth. Keeping to the race track of the newly cut grass, the familiar comforting chug of the engine and delicious smell of chopped grass as Father, pipe in mouth, manoeuvred the large Atco around the slope surrounding the pond. Suddenly they were gone; instead of the familiar chug there was a loud gurgling, hissing noise and Father went into the water shouting, 'Bugger, I've lost my pipe.' My brothers were laughing but all I remember was a feeling of terror. They told me afterwards that I kept saying, 'Grown-ups don't do that.'

Until this moment, I always believed it was Father who shaped what I became. His was the physical nurturing, the hugs and kisses and understanding when things went wrong.

Mother spanked and gave us all good clips behind the ear for no apparent reason other than the one in her own mind. Perhaps I am being unfair, for I cannot help thinking that had her generation still been around today's prison population would be reduced considerably.

My mother was well read. Her father, my grandfather, was a member of the Pen Club. My father was not well read, so I suppose I am fortunate in having inherited a balanced view of life. Just as everyone does, they brought different things to both their marriage and parenting.

Perhaps I should think more about my mother and try and bring her into focus. Unlike Father, she never hugged me. I have no idea whether she hugged my brothers, but I remember the smell of her – Craven A cigarettes and Coty face powder, which she kept in a cut-glass container with a large swansdown puff, replenishing it from time to time from a pretty round box covered in a black, white and orange circular pattern.

CHAPTER 11

Approaching Pizza Hut, pushing through the evening crowds on the wet pavement, Connor saw Miss was already seated at a window table. She waved and his heart sank, for he was hoping to avoid exposure.

Opening the door, the heat from the restaurant hit him. He was pleased to get inside after a day in the biting-cold easterly helm wind; its calling card, a ruler-straight bar of black cloud, had been resting along the Pennines for more than twenty-four hours, waiting to choose its moment.

Miss came towards him, her arms outstretched and gave him a hug. Much as it gave him pleasure, he wished that she hadn't in full view of Botchergate. And he had yet to learn to control the urges; he kept on his fluorescent jacket to conceal any embarrassment and sat down feeling awkward.

He fished in the back pocket of his jeans for the memory stick onto which he had transferred most of his old biddy's scribblings and put it on the table. Before he was able to explain things, Miss stood up and said, 'I'm just going to get myself a coffee. Can I get you anything, Connor?'

He could have eaten a horse. 'No, thanks.' He felt flustered and having to eat at the same time as explaining would be too much.

There was noise in the street outside and a banging on the

window, and what he had dreaded most was there: Seb, with his dyed pink hair, putting out his studded tongue, twiddling his fingers, a thumb in one ear, his other hand holding a can of Newcastle Brown.

Miss came back at that moment and misjudged the situation. 'I hoped, Connor, that when you left school you would break all ties with Seb. He is not a good influence.' She put down her coffee, went to the entrance, opened the door and shouted, 'Sebastian Davidson, if you don't bugger off I'll call the police.'

Connor had never seen this side of her before; in the classroom she had been subservient to the system, walking on eggshells, being politically correct to the detriment of the truth.

'You can't touch me here, you're not in school now,' Seb retorted. 'Shall I tell the headmaster about what you and Connor get up to in the evenings? You'll be in the queue at the job centre tomorrow.'

'That bloody youth. What on earth was his mother thinking, giving him the name Sebastian?' Miss laughed.

'I think it was something to do with Seb Coe winning a medal.'

She sat down again and took a deep breath. 'Well now, Connor dear. What have we here?'

'It's not all here 'cos I haven't finished reading it all, but I think someone in the old biddy's family should read it. It was obviously important to her, otherwise she wouldn't have bothered to write it.'

'That is very perceptive of you, Connor, and I admire your motivation.'

Connor was unsure what 'perceptive' meant, but he knew the word 'motivation'. Dave had used it as a word to thank him when he had done something off his own bat. He was beginning to understand the importance of words.

'Having self-motivation is far more important than passing exams.' Miss took another sip of her coffee. 'I think I mentioned that I've traced Harry's parents. You can always contact them and hand the hard drive and memory stick to them, then you will have discharged your responsibility.'

Connor thought about this for a moment. It was not what he had in mind. He was fond of the old lady; she had become a sort of reliable friend and, although he had only passed the time of day with Harry, he had taken to him, wanted to know him. Being in charge of all this stuff made him feel special; if he handed it over to the wrong people it would be like an act of treachery. And hadn't Miss once used the words 'your Harry', which made him feel good? He was a sort of James Bond on a special mission.

Miss said, tongue in cheek, 'Well, you could always volunteer for service overseas, be a VSO and request to go to Middle East and track Harry down and hand it to him personally.'

'What's a VSO, Miss?'

'It's an organisation that encourages young people to travel, visit other countries and help the less fortunate. Connor, would you allow me to transfer this onto my laptop, then I can take it home and see what your old biddy has to say?'

She took the laptop out of her bag and made the transfer. When she had finished, she said, 'I'd better get myself another coffee or they may kick us out.'

On his way home, Connor bought himself a double Mac, just in case. Gloria's suppers were unpredictable; it may be something vegan and he wasn't in the mood for lentils.

He called out hello to Gloria and went straight up to his room. He turned on the computer and Googled VSO and got a whole lot of stuff about Madagascar with pictures of black boys in a classroom. Even he knew that Madagascar was not in the Middle East. He would try again later; in the meantime, he must finish reading his old biddy stuff.

The screen flickered. She seemed happier this evening, and he smiled as he read.

***

This morning I awoke feeling quite skittish, without that debilitating feeling that I was on the last lap of life. My mind feels it is twenty-one again and ready to have a good time.

I am well aware that I need to be careful, not turn around too quickly, wait for my body to set the pace, otherwise I shall lose my balance and fall over and bump my head yet again. I am fortunate to have a skull that is either constructed like a nuclear bunker or made of foam rubber. Other than producing large lumps, it appears impervious to damage when hitting hard objects. It is the fact that I cannot pick myself up any more and need to press my emergency button yet again that has become humiliating,

The last time was three weeks ago. The whole procedure has become familiar. There I am on the floor, just coming round and wondering where the hell I am, when a detached voice calls from that small box by the phone on the hall table. My hearing isn't good enough to hear what it actually says, but the tone is reassuring so I reply as usual, 'Nothing broken. Have fallen but I can't get up.'

Within five minutes Jenny from the village, who has a key, is standing over me. The last time she sensibly brought her husband Stuart – she'd once had to go back for him as she couldn't get leverage either for her body or mine on the slippery kitchen floor.

This time I managed to slither across the kitchen onto

the hall carpet at the bottom of the stairs. The carpet gave me enough traction to push my backside on to the lowest step, but my weak wrists would take me no further. Having tried for twenty minutes, I finally pressed the red button.

It was only when Stuart arrived that it dawned on me that I was naked except for the safety alarm around my wrist. When you live on your own, not having to dress is a freedom from the expectations of others. I had been wearing my aged M&S blue-suede moccasins, my faithful travelling companions, but they had detached themselves during my fall.

In an act of chivalry, Stuart picked them up before me and gently replaced them on my feet. Standing up again and looking down, I could see he wanted to laugh. 'Now what have we got here?' There was humour in his voice, the antidote for embarrassment and the only vaccine that forestalls the pandemic of old age and death. It's better not to try to grow old graciously nor gracefully; it doesn't work.

As he looked down at the crumpled heap of bones I have become, I had to tell him about the slippers, how they had stood with me in that oven-hot cell on Robben Island, protecting me from the heat of the concrete floor. Later they had walked me along the Skeleton Coast of Namibia, its sands the resting place of whale bones bleached white by the sun, their neighbours the skeletons of ships and man's folly. I could tell he didn't believe me and thought I was delirious from the fall.

***

Connor remembered that he hadn't always believed the stories Nan used to tell. They had seemed too far-fetched – but now he believed them.

***

Got up early, six-thirtyish, to make a cup of tea. Drawing back the kitchen curtains, I encountered a pair of bare male legs halfway up a ladder leaning against the outside of the house. These were not any old legs, these were beautiful legs; the rising sun was behind them, its red glow catching the blond hairs on the muscled calves and thighs. Here was Adonis brightening my day.

Then I remembered. I had suggested to Stuart that, if ever he had a moment, the guttering around the house may be in need of a clean out of leaves before winter sets in. Being an early bird, a dawn man, he was making the most of a fine late-autumn morning.

I didn't make my presence known but took the mug of tea back to bed and thought about other legs I had known, WW2 military legs in tropical-kit khaki and naval legs in immaculate white shorts. There were black-and-white photos of them somewhere in the house.

I almost flirted with the postman when he arrived later. I had to remind myself to be seen as others saw me, a batty old woman with wild white hair and missing two front teeth. Instead I invited him in, for it was in between lockdowns. He helped me unscrew the safety top from a bottle of bleach and open a tin of tuna chunks, which my wizened hands were no longer capable of. Mother is shouting, 'Don't end a sentence with a preposition.'

The time will come when I shall be found on the floor in the corner of the kitchen wrapped in an old rug, the Kerr tartan one perhaps, which belonged to my step mother-in-law and holds its own memories and the smell of kindness. I will be like an old sheepdog who knows when its time has come and takes itself off to the corner of the barn to snuggle down amidst the familiar unwashed blankets of its life and go peacefully. I have no wish to be rehoused amongst strangers eating food out of Tupperware. I feel sorry for those who die surrounded by everything new, in the same way that I feel sadness for those elderly cats and dogs rescued in their dotage and placed in cages in animal sanctuaries waiting to be rehomed to soothe human consciences.

I have just noticed that my computer screen, keyboard and the desk in my study are covered by a thick layer of dust and crumbs. I worry that the dust may affect its workings. Can you still buy feather dusters? They would solve the problem, but I fear the animal rights people will have put a stop to them and they will be made of plastic and I shall be left with a feeling of guilt.

The helm wind is getting up again, cold, strong and familiar. I welcome it, for we have learnt to respect one another. I forgive it when it brings the odd branch down, sends my dustbin halfway down the village and denies a newborn lamb its life because I have met the helm's sisters, those warm desert winds which sculpt the wilderness of sand into beauty. Now they play skittishly with plastic bottles, dancing them across continents to clog up the oases of the planet.

Who do I tell that I don't want to be resuscitated – the butcher, the baker or the candlestick maker? I have tried with the children but they are reluctant to talk about it and say, 'You've got years to go yet, Mum.' That, of course, is the problem.

In my childhood there was a popular children's song, 'All I Want for Christmas Is My Two Front Teeth'. All I want is to be listened to, for someone to believe in me, otherwise life has been a waste of energy.

I wouldn't mind having the teeth as well.

I long to be digitally savvy, to be able to participate, contribute, question, but you cannot teach an old bitch new tricks. Give us your views, they say, and when I pick up the phone and am full of anticipation it puts me on hold and plays music.

Harry knows when I am thinking about him. There was a text message from him within the hour.

CHAPTER 12

The rapidity with which Christmas comes around has convinced me that it now happens at least three times a year. I loved Christmas when it meant something, but now it has become a bugbear, a commercial necessity to keep the economy going. The obligation to choose, write and send cards is overwhelming.

I try to keep in touch with all the left-over widows of Hugh's wartime naval days. It has become a duty; as wife of the late president of their ship's association, an all-ranks gathering plus wives, formed after the war to keep the comradeship going and to support one another, mingling is still necessary. An exchange of cards has become standard duty; they are now on my watch.

***

Connor's dad and his real mum never sent or got cards. He had noticed that Gloria got a few, which she hid from Dad. Nan always had an advent calendar sent to her by the Catholic church; it was that which had made Christmas special for Connor. He knew he was not going to wake up to a stocking at the end of the bed like children did on television. But his excitement at creeping into Nan's room early in the morning in the vest and pants in which he had slept, snuggling under her tea-stained self-knitted bed jacket, waking her up and her not minding and opening the next little window, had been sufficient to make the days before Christmas special. There were unexpected angels, mistletoe and wise men and camels and Nan explained what they were and what they meant.

He carried these images in his head for the whole day, his fingers in his ears to blot out Mum and Dad shouting. Things had improved when Gloria arrived; he had been too old for stockings, but there were crackers and roast chicken and the latest CD from Gloria.

Last Christmas, Dave had an advent calendar hanging in his kiosk at the recycling plant. He'd found it amongst the rubbish and thought he would enter into the festive spirit, but the windows had remained shut. Finally Connor had opened them; enclosed within each tiny space there was a photo of a pop star or celeb. On Christmas Day it was a picture of Madonna with a baby on her knee.

***

The first Christmas card arrived in November. It was not at all Christmassy and it was also familiar, for the sender had sent the same one before, a painting of an impressive Herefordshire bull owned by David, a final survivor of the ship's company. I prayed that this year he had included an address, because last year I had tried to get in touch with him and failed.

His surname is Williams, and he is one of many stokers of that name who survived two torpedo attacks. He was one of the lucky ones who was blasted from the furnace heat of the engine room into the icy waters of the North Sea, gulping surface oil, rescued by miracle. His mates below decks less fortunate. The men in the engine room were always the last escapees as the water burst through the hatches, and they drowned in a shroud of boiling steam as the ship went down.

David never married and had no close relatives. In civilian life he was a livestock farmer, breeding pedigree Hereford cattle. We got on well. He lived somewhere on the banks of the river Wye and enjoyed fishing for salmon in its waters.

There was no address. By now he must be in an old people's home. Like me, he is well into his nineties and probably experiencing the same emotions. It is not death that we fear but the thought that we may not be remembered. All our good experiences of life – the kindnesses, love, sacrifices – might be picked over by strangers searching for faults.

I spent the morning looking up old people's homes in Hereford. I made a list of their telephone numbers and sat down, intending to spend the afternoon tracking down David; it was not going to be easy because I didn't understand the irrationality of the Data Protection Act.

Before I started on the care homes, I Googled the producers of the card, the Hereford Cattle Society, hoping they would help. Ill-at-ease with modern communications, I phoned; my generation prefer it that way.

The answer was mechanical but I held on in the hope of getting a human connection. A call out of the blue didn't go down well with the girl on the switchboard; her lilting sing-song Welsh accent had a hint of annoyance in it as she asked if she could help.

'We have dozens of members called David Williams. What is his address?'

'That is what I hoped you may be able to help me with.'

'Oh, we don't give out people's addresses willy-nilly. There are data protection laws, you know.'

I put down the phone and started on the list of old people's homes. I had an hour to spare and, aware that I might be in for the long haul, I settled down comfortably, making sure I had reading glasses, pencil and paper and a large whisky at the ready. After ten minutes the whisky was gone, and after three fruitless calls I gave up. Wasn't the twenty-first century meant to be the new Age of Enlightenment?

I had written down what I would say, giving as much information about David as possible: 'I am trying to track down an elderly gentleman by the name of David Williams. He and my late husband were in the Navy together.' At that stage there was usually a metallic click and I was transferred to a different voice so had to start again. I tried a different tack: 'Do you by any chance have a gentleman by the name of David Williams? He will be in his late nineties, a bachelor and retired livestock farmer who lived on the banks of the Wye?'

I would have been happy with a simple yes or no but got, 'I am afraid because of data protection we cannot divulge that information.'

I poured myself another large whisky and felt guilty because it was only 11.30am.

I had the same problem a fortnight later in the waiting room of the doctor's surgery. An elderly couple were just leaving. Their faces were familiar but I was at a loss to put a name to them. They greeted me like a long-lost friend. 'What a lovely surprise to see you again after all these years.'

After they left, I asked the receptionist to remind me who they were. 'I'm afraid I am not allowed to tell you,' she said.

'Data protection?' I asked.

She nodded. She was half smiling; we both saw the lunacy of the situation.

I am unsure what or who data protection is protecting; it is certainly not the elderly because it is just adding to our confusion.

No wonder there is so much dementia. We are being taught to lose our minds. Now the only person I can talk to openly, without censor, surcharge or restrictions put upon His time, is God. Of course He has always been there, but now people prefer a visit to the doctor.

I could no longer remember why I had picked up the phone in the first place. Who on earth had I been phoning? Was it one of the children?

I walked into the kitchen and saw the card with the painting of the Hereford Bull lying on the table and remembered. It was a magnificent animal, deep copper coloured and white, a perfect conformation like Ferdinand, a Simmental bull I once knew and loved. He was honey coloured and white, and came into my life all those years ago when Hugh and I had tried our hand at farming after Hugh had turned his back on the Navy and industry. Once I was considered quite an authority on cattle, not that mad old woman who lives on the edge of the village.

I find it quite amusing that during my last conversation with the lovely Scottish cardiologist who now keeps an eye on my heart she said, 'Nothing wrong with the plumbing of your heart. It's the electrics.'

I have just received a card from Anna to say that she has bought me a share in a race horse for Christmas. Share is not quite the right word; a more accurate description would be one of its fetlocks. This has cheered me up no end, for usually it is lavender-scented soap or bedroom slippers.

There are twenty or so other local owners. Some names I recognise from my youth, county family types still going strong from the days of the Yellow Earl and cap doffing. We are all being invited to choose a name for our new acquisition, a two-year-old green filly from a thoroughbred breeder in Ireland. Her dam has form. She is to go into training at the local racing stables just across the village green from the church where Father gave me away to Hugh. I have been informed that my filly's dam preferred hard going, so hopefully her daughter will be a stayer.

I looked up at the sky and told Father all about her. I am certain I heard him call down and say, 'Put a tenner on her for me,' just like in the old days. So strongly do I feel his presence that I had to open the back door to let out the smoke from his pipe. He would be 123 years old but he is just as much alive to me as he ever was.

This week I am thinking about him more than ever. A new film has just come out about the First World War. Father was shot down by the Germans, his flimsy Sopworth Camel crashing to the ground and him with his hands in the air being captured at the age of seventeen. The smell of his wet tweeds and pipe are far more real than the flickering of celluloid.

I managed to stay awake until 9pm to watch the final episode of an adaptation of Nancy Mitford's *The Pursuit of Love*. What joy! Suddenly I was back in Paris again, with the freedom of spirit that city exudes. But where have all the Fabrice de Sauvaterres gone? Gone to political correctness, every one.

Remembering the indiscretions of youth makes old age tolerable, but only if you are prepared to live with the guilt.

CHAPTER 13

Since the debacle of data protection, I am determined to reorganise my life and take control of it. I have sidelined things for far too long. Life has become a cliché: 'never put off until tomorrow what can be done today' has become 'better late than never'. And I have just woken to the knowledge that I don't know who I am. This has happened a few times before. The best way to deal with it has been to sit down wherever I am and take stock.

I have started making lists, things to remember before I retire so as not to retrace my steps and give the children and grandchildren the ammunition they need to insist upon installing a stairlift. Hugh wouldn't approve of a stairlift and they will still need his consent; he may have been dead for decades but he still holds sway. He would say that a stairlift will spoil the look of the staircase. I can console myself with the thought that exercising my joints will prevent me contracting 'bungalow knees'.

I lock the back door, make certain my mobile is charged, put the landline phone back on its charger, select a banana for tomorrow's breakfast in bed, get a jug of water, make certain the commode, my trusty steed, is correctly positioned for a quick mounting in the dark. Its sturdy handles remind me of the pommel on a saddle.

Another contemporary has died. Funerals have become my most constant form of social contact and entertainment. They are performances witnessed from the back pews of churches on uncomfortably hard seats. People gather to support one another's grief and perhaps, a little late in the day, get to know the deceased better through the thoughts of others. Funerals are also a challenge for weak bladders; forward planning is necessary

After Covid, I made a decision. For the next five years, I will only bid a formal farewell to those I hope will come and say farewell to me if the time of our departures is reversed. This has been an enormous weight off my mind. Living in a small rural community, there are occasions when your presence is necessary. There are tenuous connections with neighbours; fields adjoining, rights of way, and sharing a muck spreader can be a stronger reason for attending a funeral than being a blood relative.

In the same way, I tried to avoid tedious corporate cocktail parties in those heady days when Hugh insisted I attend because some business deal might depend upon me putting in an appearance. Sometimes, to my surprise, I quite enjoyed them and met interesting people with things on their minds other than profit-and-loss accounts.

So it is with funerals. My hearing aid allows me to drop in on the conversations of others. 'Who was the vicar going on and on about? That wasn't the woman I knew – she must have mistaken her for someone else, got the names mixed up. It's easily done, I imagine. She is the last person on earth I would call kind hearted and loved by all who knew her. She was a thoroughly unpleasant, vindictive woman. Do you remember how she treated poor Gladys…' And with that, they disappear to the village hall for cheap white wine and home-made scones, their host quickly forgotten.

But there have been performances for dear ones that were so deeply moving that I wept throughout and never gave my bladder a thought.

Weak bladders do have unexpected advantages; in the middle of the night they take on the role of alarm clocks, never requiring a new battery or having to be reset. Mine wakes me every two hours, almost on the hour. Sometimes I am sufficiently wide awake to turn on the TV, which is placed decadently at the foot of the bed, and watch fascinating programmes about the planet.

Only this morning there was one called *In Too Deep* – or was it *Out of Your Depth*. I can't quite remember. It was one of those environmentally friendly documentaries that reaffirm something my generation and those before have always known since time immemorial, that the oceans are sacred, secret places of magic and awe to be gently paddled in when you are very little, swum in when you are a little bigger, fished in, gazed upon and sailed on should you be fortunate to know someone with a boat.

Then along comes the next generation, hailed as the new messiahs with their miracles of plastic and microchips and globalisation. And now I have grandchildren and great-grandchildren trying to reverse things yet again. They are obsessed by colour – black, white, brown, yellow. When they are not turning pink, they are going green.

The programme informed me that sinister things are happenings beneath the waves. Permission has been granted to mine the seabed for cobalt, something that is needed in order to replace fossil fuels and make everyone feel righteous.

Could I have dreamt the whole thing? Was it all a nightmare? I know nothing of cobalt other than it is a blue colour much favoured by artists. I was totally unaware that it is an element necessary to produce batteries, and batteries are needed to keep everything up and running now that coal has got the thumbs down.

Shall I tell Crispin? He has just bought an electric car at great expense, the first in the village. I really don't want to disillusion him, for he truly does try and he goes on Extinction Rebellion marches. I try to tell him he is wasting his time; two decades ago I joined half a million people and marched through London trying to keep the countryside free from urban ignorance. That didn't work, either.

I am reminded of something Mother once read at bedtime: 'Always keep a hold of nurse, for fear of finding something worse.' Is that Edward Lear or Hilaire Belloc? I shall have to go downstairs and look it up, otherwise it will prey on my mind. I shall look up cobalt at the same time.

I gleaned the information about cobalt from my beloved *Hamlyn's* with the help of the magnifying glass that belonged to my mother. I located cobalt on page 323 between an exquisite engraving of a coati (*Nasau narica*) and cobber (Australian slang for 'mate'), followed by William Cobbet (1753–1835, journalist and politician).

I really shouldn't go downstairs in the middle of the night. If I fall, it causes my kind neighbours inconvenience and my children and grandchildren a lot of hassle. I got myself safely back into bed. The TV was still blaring the news yet again, this time a landing on Mars. Why cannot we leave other planets alone, leave them to our imagination? 'Fly me to the moon, let me play among the stars, let me know what life is like on Jupiter and Mars...'

I am pretty certain that, if there is life on Jupiter and Mars, we must be the neighbours from hell. I know I am being a curmudgeon and what has been achieved technically by superior brains is awesome in its truest sense, but because I don't understand the brilliance behind the technology doesn't mean I can't condemn it. It's like all those fashion models who banned foxhunting.

If life exists on other planets, perhaps they are watching us this very minute. Maybe they assume that cars, because of their proliferation and mobility, are the animate inhabitants of earth and that humans live as parasites within them.

Couldn't get to sleep again and my mind has gone into overdrive.

I am allowing the wokes to get to me. All generations think they know better than their predecessors, but the present lot are particularly vicious in destroying the minds and memories of a multitude of octogenarians. Self-certainties spew out minute by minute; a quick click and they have read it, said it all and influenced another session of bad government.

***

Although Connor did not fully understand what his old biddy was yattering on about, it felt kind of right. Nan used to talk like that, say the same sort of stuff but in a different way.

He wondered whether he was getting to the end of her writing. He would keep going until the words ran out.

What was it Miss had said about helping people in other countries? It might be easier being kind to people you didn't know. How old did you have to be to get a passport? He would ask Dave.

***

Being mistaken for someone else has happened a few times in my life. Sometimes it turned out to be rather fun. Once it was intentional, when my American host wanted to impress his guests. He was some billionaire in Beverley Hills who had made his money out of Heaven only knows what and was hoping to clinch a deal with the company for which Hugh worked. He had introduced me as Lady Lancaster from Goode Olde England, and I enjoyed playing the role for the evening.

With hindsight, another was a rather sad little affair for the person who made the mistake, although I rather enjoyed his error. I was flattered when a total stranger came up and asked me to dance; Hugh never danced, and on social old-boy occasions I had learnt to play second fiddle. Normally I would have declined, but it was one of those rare evenings when I felt good. I had bought a long dress which I felt happy in, something I would never waste money on normally but it was a formal black-tie do. It never occurred to me for one moment that the man was asking me to dance because he thought I was someone else.

It was one of those public-school parties, a centenary reunion to raise funds. We had gone because Hugh still felt affectionate about his old boarding school. I couldn't get away quickly enough from mine.

After sherry and general mingling, we were seated for dinner at a circular table for eight. I was enjoying that blissful experience of old-style chivalry, when men stood up when you entered a room and chairs were pulled out for you before a meal. Of course these things still happen, but rarely instinctively; the feminist movement has seen to that. I gather they teach etiquette at university now and you can get a degree in hospitality.

What was I thinking about before feminism distracted me?

It was a relief to leave the man sitting on my left at dinner.

He was quite heavy going; it was only when I got him talking about himself that I realised he was a bigwig. I glanced at his place card but couldn't decipher his name. There was certainly a Sir at the front.

It was then that my knight came and asked me to dance.

I was enjoying the quickstep when my partner congratulated me on my husband's appointment as a governor of the school. I tried to absorb this information, for it seemed unlikely. I had left Hugh deep in his familiar killjoy conversation with the person on his right, who I presumed was Lady Bigwig. It was only when my partner brought his son into the conversation – his name was Nigel and he was in the Middle Sixth – that I realised that I was being subjected to political pressure. He thought *I* was Lady Bigwig. A contribution to the school was on offer should Nigel become a prefect.

Everything happens for a reason and has its consequences. To be mistaken for someone married to a man who was successful in the eyes of the world was rather nice. It boosted my ego. I had my moment of glorious bliss, which is worth an age without a name, even though my knight hadn't the grace to walk me back to my table when he realised his faux pas. I was chuckling inside and squirming for his embarrassment. I wonder whether his son was made head boy. I hope not. Nigel will be in his sixties by now.

As I was sitting down again, Lady Bigwig caught my eye. It was a practiced eye, and it was clear she had read the situation correctly.

I woke early this morning as usual, my body programmed not only by my bladder but years of being on duty at dawn to help animals giving birth, blowing and slapping breath into seemingly lifeless bodies. But those days are long gone. Instead I check emails which have arrived overnight, go back to bed with a mug of tea, hunker down under the feather duvet and yearn for a body to hug. The voice of Bob Dylan was offering me a warm embrace to make me feel his love. It reminded me of those moments of love and infidelity which created a lifetime's guilt and moments of pure joy. I try not to think about them.

Instead I turned on Channel 4 and watched *Frasier* and, because I am fortunate to still be uncured of joy, I had a bloody good belly laugh. My beloved brothers used to say it is only true humour if you really cannot stop laughing and the beer comes back through your nose.

Easter is coming up. Is there enough whisky in the house to see me through the crucifixion of Christ?

CHAPTER 14

Icannot believe I am still alive because last night I was with my parents. They were as they must have been when I was still in the womb, Dad in his plus fours and brown trilby, pipe in hand, Mum, flat chested in a cloche hat, smoking a Craven A. Their smell is still with me, their scent still on the pillow. Mother was standing over me saying, 'Time to get up and wash the sleepy-peeps out of your eyes.'

I didn't want to get up; if I left their presence I might never find them again, they might never return. But I had to – Morrison's were delivering and the back door was still locked

Perhaps God is giving me some extra time, giving me a second chance to see things differently, a *raison d'être*. Could it be that my recent habit of jotting down the things that come unexpectedly into my head now has significance?

Enough of all that. The priority at that moment was getting myself safely into my knickers so that I could answer the knock on the door with some decorum. I have got it down to a fine art: I sit on edge of bed, bend down slowly to avoid dizzy spells and guide my left foot into what looks like an opening. The left foot is always the one to take the first step, but today my little toe caught on something – a hole, where a hole should not be. My knickers are wearing out.

Tugging didn't help but seemed to make my toe and

knickers hold onto each other more tightly. I realised that the overgrown nail on my left small toe had become entwined in the fraying cotton of my knickers and only a surgical operation was likely to part them. That involved a trip to the bathroom where I thought I had left the scissors.

I walked along the landing, my foot dragging the knickers, but when I arrived I forgot why I was there and cleaned my remaining teeth instead.

An eye for an eye, a tooth for a tooth. Love thy neighbour and forgive us our trespasses. Turn the other cheek. The phrases are swimming around in my mind.

It is one of the greatgrandchildren's birthdays tomorrow and I have forgotten to send a card, let alone a present. You have to be so careful with presents nowadays because they can be misinterpreted. I would love to send her a copy of *Little Black Sambo* but that might cause friction.

I so wish the family would forget my birthday. The next one is within striking distance. Why, oh why, do they feel it necessary to keep reminding me of those numbers which I don't feel?

They have just asked me what I would like for my birthday. Usually it is a meal out, but my lack of appetite makes it hardly worth the effort so I said, in all seriousness, that I want a copy of the Koran. I am finding the Bible too contradictory and thought maybe the Koran would send out a simpler message to explain the meaning of life.

A family member replied, 'Do you want it in Arabic?' They may have intended to sound amusing, but there was sarcasm in the voice. It was a mistake to confide in others; later I found them in the dining room, deep in conversation with low voices. Unfortunately I had put a new battery in my hearing aid and heard quite distinctly, 'She's finally gone senile.'

I would like to have retaliated and told them that I had been thinking about belief and faith for some time. I have even been to the reference library and tried to peruse *The Oxford Dictionary of World Religions* edited by John Bowker, which is deemed a comprehensive and reliable source. Unfortunately the sheer weight of the book defeated me and my old wrists were incapable of lifting it from the shelf. My late-in-the-day thirst for knowledge crashed to the ground amidst looks of disapproval.

Anyway, this morning my priority was still to get my knickers on. Knickers and the Koran were whizzing about together in my head. In my *Hamlyn's Encyclopaedic World Dictionary* two pages separate them and over a hundred interesting words: *knobkerrie, koilonychias and Korandi.*

I sat on the loo seat and managed to cut through the offending toenail to release my knickers. At my age it isn't worth buying new ones; no one is going to see them unless I am hit by a bus and rushed to hospital and then it will be too late to care. Mother would disapprove. As children, we were taught always to be aware of the cleanliness of our underwear.

Throughout my life my brothers have ribbed me for an incident that happened when I was seven or eight. I was still at first school with my youngest brother; my two elder brothers were already at boarding school.

It was a rushed Monday morning school day. Mother called, 'Clean knickers in the linen cupboard.' In the rush, and with Father shouting 'time to go' on the half-hour journey to school where he dropped us off on his way to work, I forgot to put them on.

I can still feel the cold blast as the car door opened and the horror of the situation became clear. The only things saving me from nudity was a short liberty bodice, blouse and gymslip.

Even worse, it was gym that day when blouses had to be tucked into knickers. I refused to get out of the car.

Father was totally out of his depth but my brother was relishing the situation. He raced into school to share my plight with everyone. Word of my knickerless-ness spread throughout the school.

Father asked me whether I knew which shops sold knickers because he had a meeting at 9.30 and there wasn't time to go home. I remember suggesting a small shop into which Mother had once taken me. It sold pretty things and the lady behind the counter smiled.

My nose was the height of the counter. Father stood by the door, refusing to participate further. 'I forgot to put my knickers on this morning,' I said.

'We'll see what we can do. We don't sell children's clothes but we may have an extra-small pair of ladies' undergarments.'

I had already realised that the knickers in the glass case counter didn't look like the kind you tucked your blouse into, but they were all that were on offer. Father paid for them and we left.

Sniggering greeted my arrival at school as I crept into the girls' lavatories to put them on. Where there should have been elastic, there were pretty lacy bits – and I was not allowed to participate in gymnastics. It was on that day that I learnt to laugh at myself. It is just as well, for it helped me get through all those challenging years of being married to dear old Hugh.

I can relive every moment of that day but now I cannot remember what month it is. Memory and forgetfulness are getting all shook up, as Elvis would have it. I'm not a great Elvis fan but he may have enlightened a different generation. I prefer Dylan; he sweeps the mind clean of old debris and, if I play it loud enough, attracts callers like the postmen. Dylan's music persuades them to pop their head round the door and listen for a minute. They respond to his teachings as the church's followers drain away.

Oh God, Morrison's are banging on the door. I shall have to go down in my dressing gown. I hope it is Stella – she is understanding.

***

Gloria heard Connor laughing and called up, 'Hope you're not getting up to mischief.' Gloria's calls were always lovely and caring: 'Hope you had a good day, supper ready in a mo.'

But his mind was listening to his old lady and he didn't answer. He kept on reading.

***

How is it that I have suddenly acquired an enquiring mind in the tenth decade of my life? I am absolutely certain that last fall did it. It was a lovely sunny day and I ventured out without my stick. I lost my balance and went down, hitting my head on the old stone garden trough. As I went down, I noticed the tulips were coming up. I had bought three hundred mixed ones and planted them everywhere, something to look forward to in the spring.

Was it that bump on the head that stopped time, sent my memory into reverse, back to the L-plate days that made those Sunday morning phone calls with my eldest brother David such a joy?

I feel I should be sharing this knowledge with someone. Perhaps we all need a bloody good bump on the head. I have a great-niece who is reading neuroscience at Cardiff University; should I tell her? But, fearing ridicule, I hesitate and keep quiet.

I have no idea how long I lay there, but when the warmth of the sun brought me round its position in relation to earth had moved. The back of my head sported a painful lump the size of a tennis ball and I am pretty certain that something within my brain had shifted. It was my road to Damascus; as I lay there, I could hear David playing jazz on the old upright piano in our childhood nursery. I managed to pull myself up by clutching the side of the trough and pushing a foot against a protruding cobblestone.

David is approaching his centenary three hundred miles away in a care home on the Somerset Levels, and I am approaching mine rejoicing in the hills of the north. The distance and infirmities that separate us make the likelihood of us ever meeting up again remote. The pattern for the past ten years has been that every Sunday, at 10.30 a m, sharp, we take turns to foot the telephone bill and have a chat. It has replaced matins. In all that time we have never missed a Sunday, although there have been one or two late calls when both our bladders had got the upper hand.

We always greet one another in our local dialect. 'Hoosta ga'an on, lass?' The answer is dependent on what sort of week I have had: 'nobbut fair' or 'graidly'. Then we talk, reminisce about an idyllic childhood lived within the restrictions of war.

One Sunday David said, 'Do you remember Mrs Bombinaiphoff?'

It was like an explosion in my head, like a land mine going off, but instead of destruction the name stirred up long hidden feelings of innocence and fun, when happiness came naturally. David has faith in who he is; he learnt early how life worked for him, whilst I never did. I see both sides of every argument, which makes me indecisive. Hugh used to say, 'For God's sake, woman, make up your mind.'

Mrs Bombinaiphoff was an invention of our childhood imagination. More real to us than our parents, Mrs Bombinaiphoff solved our problems and listened.

***

Connor sensed that things were coming to an end, that finally the words would run out and he must decide what to do, take positive steps to get all this to its rightful owner. He had bought a second memory stick so that, when the time came, he could transfer the lot. That seemed to be the best idea.

***

Now the phone is dead on Sunday mornings. David had his own fall and couldn't get up. He died in hospital twelve days later. We did manage to speak once more. He was a favourite with the nurses and they fixed up a phone for him, the NHS at its most palliative.

I said, 'Hoosta ga'an on, lad?' and he said, 'Nobbut middlin.' I can still hear the chuckle in his voice.

And then he said, his voice faint and breathless, 'Do you remember Thompson and the septic tank? It must have been between the wars.'

It was one of those apocryphal family anecdotes which held some truth. Thompson had been with the family for years as gardener, handyman and general dogsbody. He was also in charge of the septic tank.

Whether he was being bloody-minded (which he could be), or whether he just hadn't thought things through, he decided to clean it out on the day of Mother's garden party in aid of the Red Cross. The septic tank was a good quarter of a mile from the house, so it didn't really matter. Garden parties were not his scene but responsibility for the septic tank was, and he had found a blockage and needed to inform his employers

He had walked up to the house. Mother was in the garden, surrounded by the great and the good of the county, giving her speech of welcome. She saw Thompson approaching and asked, 'Is there a problem?'

He announcing to all and sundry with true Cumbrian honesty, 'Seesta, tho's bin usin' far ower much peaper.'

That was the last laugh David and I shared. His last words on this earth were, 'Do you remember Bronco?'

Not all my beloved brothers died laughing. I pray I may be awarded that privilege.

***

Connor felt a great desire to hug his old lady tightly.

CHAPTER 15

Woke up this morning with a delicious sense of joy. The end has not come and I am feeling better than I have for weeks. It is another lovely autumn day and the clocks go back tonight. A time for bedding down under the duvet and planting bulbs, making certain there will be colour to look forward to next spring when the clocks go forward again

Most wonderful of all was a text from Anna to say she has heard from Harry. He phoned her to update her. He is now at the UNICEF headquarters in Amman, having a break and doing a bit of admin work. Thank God he is away from Assad's bombs. Perhaps I sensed his safety and that is why I woke up feeling good.

Abrinet awaits their second child. She plans to return to the camp to give birth alongside the refugees for whom she cares. Harry is a bit concerned but, as he says, Abrinet is made of sterner stuff. They both plan to return to Syria, where they are desperately short of doctors and help of every kind. Sen may stay in Amman to continue his schooling; he will reach adulthood bilingual – what a precious gift.

My time is running out but I don't want to go until I have met Abrinet, the love of Harry's life. How wonderful that he has found such contentment. It is just as well that Hugh died when he did; he would not have taken kindly to a mixed-race marriage in the family. There was all that hoo-ha when his brother married a Dutch girl on the rebound from being in a German POW camp and they went to live with her family in Jamaica.

***

Reading this, Connor knew that he must get a move on. Whatever he did, he was going to do it on his own, make his own decisions. He now knew where Harry was and could write him a letter. If they needed helpers he was ready, and it didn't matter how dirty the jobs were – all the men in his family were used to dirty work.

He wondered whether he would ever meet the love of his life. The odds were pretty long at the moment; he hadn't liked his real mother, though he was fond of Gloria, and he felt no attraction for the girls at school. When he thought about it, the only person he really liked was Miss. If she wasn't there he really would miss her but, as she was seven years older than him, he tried not to think about it. Nan had been in an altogether different category of love.

He was unsure how he should address Harry. *Hi Harry*, the way he would address his smartphone friends, didn't sound quite right. He decided he would do what his Nan would have done and start the letter with *Dear Sir* or *Dear Dr O'Brien*, and enclose a stamped addressed envelope.

The day at work seemed long and he couldn't wait to get home. There was a pad of paper in the kitchen which Gloria used for reminders or shopping lists; he could tear a couple of sheets from that and do a rough copy first, for he had to say the right words. Writing thoughts down was more difficult than thinking them; that was why he had failed his English GCSE.

150

He would have liked to confide in Miss and tell her his plans, but she would say think about it, sleep on in it. But thinking about things was what you were taught in school; they taught you to accept things that you didn't feel. Before he left he would text her.

He started writing, having plumped for *Dear Sir*.

You won't remember me but I met you at the recycling plant outside Carlisle where I work about a year ago when you told me you had been cleaning out your Nan's house who had died and you chucked out a computer and you were in a hurry cos you had a plane to catch. I know I shouldn't have cos it's against the rules but I took the hard drive out of that computer and read what was on it and its all sorts of stuff written by your Nan which is sort of cool and interesting and I thought you might like to have it. Addressed envelope enclosed, I would have put a stamp on it but don't have the right kind.

From Connor O'Grady

Next morning he went to the post office to get an application form for a passport and asked how much to send a letter to Amman. He pronounced it incorrectly; the man behind the counter thought he said Annan which was just over the border. 'The usual second-class stamp will do.'

There had been a bit of a discussion, so Connor showed him the envelope and pointed to the word 'Amman'.

The man behind the counter said, 'Oh, you mean Amman in Jordan. Off to join ISIS, are we?' He looked up the correct postage, licked the stamp, thumped it onto the letter with his fist and slipped it into the bag behind him.

Connor had difficulty understanding the passport form, but quickly understood that he was going to have to find £85 from somewhere. On minimum wage it was going to take a bit of time to get it together; he would have to cut down on the

Coke and stuff.

He asked Dave if there was any chance of some overtime. Dave liked to keep the overtime to himself because it paid double, but his sanguine disposition worked upon his natural generosity and he offered Connor his next early-morning Sunday stint. 'Got a girlfriend or something?' He winked and added, 'Doing you a favour. You know I have kids and a missus to support.'

Connor knew that he hadn't. Dave had once confided in him, saying, 'I never had kids. The missus and me couldn't seem to manage it.'

Connor thought about how he had been conceived without thought, unwanted.

In the end he had to bring Gloria into his plans because he needed his birth certificate, or at least a copy of it. Like life, his explanation was all white lies and half-truths. 'I'm joining up with a few mates for a trip to Amsterdam.'

Probably the truth would have been easier to explain. Gloria had wheedled his birth certificate out of Dad without letting on; she'd given him a cock-and-bull story that, as Connor's stepmother, she should have a copy just in case. She helped Connor fill in the passport application form and told him that she was pleased that he had some friends.

After a week Connor, started looking out for the post. His passport arrived more quickly than expected, but he was anxious that if Gloria saw a letter addressed to him in his own writing with a foreign stamp, she might smell a rat and think he was into drugs. When the letter did arrive, it was wedged between the usual junk mail, which Gloria had not bothered to look at and had thrown onto the bottom step of the stairs.

He sat down on his bed and tore open the envelope.

Dear Connor,

I was pleased to receive your letter. I do indeed remember you – you were most helpful and my wife Abrinet remembers asking you about your job. I would be most interested to have the hard drive and any information you can download. It was remiss of me not to check before throwing away the computer. Thank you for rescuing it.

I was very close to my grandmother and remember towards the end of her life she started putting down her thoughts and memories. In fact, it became quite an obsession. She always tried to give sound advice and now I wish I had listened to her more.

I may be in the UK shortly, and will be coming north to arrange the sale of Gran's house, so I will make contact again. It would be unwise to send the material electronically – it might get lost in the magnitude of emergency calls we receive.

Again my thanks.

Yours sincerely, Harry O'Brien

Beneath the signature was a mobile number. Connor felt emboldened.

His old lady was still talking.

***

The thought that I may have got a few things right has kept me going but now my mind is questioning everything and I am unable to stop it. Even the beta blockers don't help. I know my mind is not doing it for malicious reasons, it is just trying to put the record straight. There is something to be said for the old confessional and the last rites.

Crispin phoned – if a call comes between 10.20 and 10.40 on a Monday morning it is almost always Crispin asking if he may come over and if there is anything I need. That he and Amanda came to live next door to me is an enormous blessing; they have become my unofficial carers and I rely on them more and more. And now Crispin was sitting at my kitchen table telling me they were planning to return south. What a bombshell. Without their kindness, I may not be able to continue living in the place I love.

They have given country living a try but feel they have been misled. What they are experiencing is not what is portrayed on TV, and now Amanda is yearning for the theatres and the crowded bustle of metropolitan life. They have found living in such close proximity to cattle too much of a challenge, just as the evacuees did who lived in my home at the start of the war. They returned to the East End of London too soon, and were killed in the Blitz.

I won't worry Anna with this news…

***

Connor sensed that his old lady was coming to the end of saying what she had to say, just as his Nan had. He would keep reading until her words ran out, but he now knew what he must do.

Harry's letter had been friendly. Connor would write to him again offering his services, and book a flight to Amman. Whatever Harry's reply was, he planned to go. He would have to give in his notice and say goodbye to Dave, which would be difficult, but he knew that if he didn't do it now he never would. It was like finding the courage to put your hand up in class.

CHAPTER 16

Tomorrow I think I shall be ninety-eight. Somewhere this is not in dispute; it is recorded officially, as though I were of some importance.

My mind is kicking against this officialdom, for I am aware that the next notification will be of my death. I am not ready to go just yet, though I weary at the effort of dressing and undressing, and some mornings I wake up looking forward to meeting my maker.

I dread death not for my own sake, for I am quite looking forward to no longer having to make decisions. It is just what it will put my family through, the great kerfuffle – and then there will be the question of the Will, which I suspect may cause problems.

Oh, they will ask so many questions. What did she want? Did she mention music? Had she a favourite hymn? Why can they not toss me on a bonfire and have done with it?

Now we have come out of lockdown, a church service will be allowed, but I am beginning to feel the bonfire option is preferable. It will be much less hassle for everyone, as long as they get it going and don't let me smoulder. I could include in my funeral instructions: 'Pour a bit of WD40 on the pyre – there's a tin in the garage. Let me go out with a whoosh.'

Hugh would have known how to do it. In his last days, he

enjoyed bonfires, burning the trimmings from hedge laying, returning to the house looking almost content and carrying the autumn smells of smoke and dead leaves.

I know a time will come when I don't want to live any more. Today I made the decision to throw away my beloved blue M&S moccasins. They have never let me down and I enjoyed the familiarity of their shabbiness but, like me, they have come adrift. The soles have detached from the uppers and they caught the step as I was coming downstairs. I nearly went a purler.

I thanked my moccasins for all the good times we have had together and placed them in the blue bag provided by Eden District Council. It was a sad parting.

Had I been allowed to choose the time of my going, it would have been yesterday evening when I was sitting outside in the fading sun, wrapped in rugs, following a visit from Alastair and his parents. How fortunate I am to have great-grandchildren. They live in the south and their visits are rare, even more so during lockdown. The last time Alastair was with me was just before his third birthday, yet he remembered me and spontaneously gave me a great big hug.

Some say they can remember their time in the womb. As I grow older I am not disinclined to believe them.

I had arranged an impromptu treasure hunt in the garden. There was no treasure, just some old, battered, paintless Dinky cars which I had found in the boxroom, leftovers from my son's childhood in the 1950s.

Alistair came to me for the clues, his eyes full of excitement and anticipation, jumping up and down, listening carefully, understanding, wanting to be off like a race horse at the starting gate.

'Find some blue flowers,' I said. 'They are called bluebells and you may find something hidden amongst them.'

I watched him explore and, when he found the bluebells and the hidden Morris Minor, I knew it wasn't the treasure that gave him the pleasure but the fact that he had succeeded in finding it.

The family left after tea. As the car drove away down the drive, the phone rang. Normally I never get to it before it stops ringing. I picked it up and, still in my second childhood, said, 'Hello, this is Greystoke 27,' as I had been taught to do from the age of three.

It was an aggressive foreign voice telling me I had problems with my BT connection and that I must do something immediately to rectify them. I very nearly agreed, but then I remembered the warnings of the family so I said, 'I no longer trust you,' and put down the phone. I wondered who there was left to believe in.

At that moment the phone rang again and I answered it with my newfound voice of suspicion.

'Hello, Auntie Julia.'

I tried to remember the voice.

'It's me, Auntie Julia – Liz, your goddaughter. Now we are coming out of lockdown, Richard and I would love to come over to say hello. We're happy to stand outside on the cobbles and have a quick chat, remember old times. We'll wear masks.'

Old times are all that is left. A time to come clean, when memories turn into misunderstandings and it is difficult to accept the truth. Also, I'm not into wearing masks –they remind me of my responsibilities as a child, making certain the curtains were drawn during the blackout before lights were switched on, stumbling around in the dark if I left it too late, ghosts and terror hiding around every corner.

The past few days have been interesting. Some moments I feel lucid and everything is clear and positive; other times everything seems contradictory. I suppose that is why I so enjoyed lockdown; at last I met all the right people, the people who added joy to my life through normal acts of decency.

I am missing the solitude of lockdown when I had an excuse for not doing things. My dear friend, who knows me too well, feels the same. She used to come and do the ironing and a bit of dusting so that my daughters didn't tut-tut me. We have both learnt to live with our own thoughts. I shall put her off coming for as long as possible because I am enjoying the cobwebs; they appear overnight and catch the flies, so I don't need fly papers or chemical sprays. Vera is keen on aerosols – no wonder she has asthma.

The spiders are all shapes and sizes, as are their cobwebs which vary in texture, some strong enough to capture wasps and bluebottles, others less demanding and happy with the odd fly.

The downstairs loo has become a tower block of webs, a labyrinth of construction, the foundations laid in the crevices of the sandstones steps that once led down to the coal bunker of the old house before its makeover. Now it has a smart loo and basin and Laura Ashley wallpaper, but it is still home to insects of which the spiders are aware. There are cracks in the sandstone where beetles, woodlice, centipedes, silver fish and other creepie crawlies live that only David Attenborough would recognise. They have made their home with me and, if I sit long enough on the loo, they come out to keep me company. I want to warn them about the spiders – 'He's behind you, he's behind you'. There is a whole eco system down there; perhaps I should invite one of those wildlife programmes to take photos.

Another day to get through. I have tried yet again to impress upon my children and grandchildren, please, please do not celebrate my physical age. Please, please ask my daughter-in-law not to bake me another cake. I really haven't the physical strength to blow out the candles and can no longer eat carbohydrates after 3pm without waking with acid seeping up through my oesophagus, waking me in order to reach for the Rennies, and at the same time letting go my bladder. Oesophagus and bladder both needing attention, interrupting what is going on in my mind.

Why is it assumed that all old people will eventually go doolally or take up knitting or dream about flying spitfires again, with a bit of ballroom dancing in between and reaching for the wet wipes every five minutes? Cleanliness is next to godliness; even that has been misconstrued, the word misinterpreted over the ages. 'Cleanse the thoughts of our hearts by the inspiration of Thy Holy Spirit' has turned itself into wash your hands regularly and sing 'Happy Birthday to You'.

At least I know the true origin of the word 'doolally'. I learnt that from Hugh's father from his time stationed in India in the 1930s; it was British army slang for the town of, Deolali where the army sanatorium was situated.

When members of his company became ill or were wounded, they were sent to the sanatorium at Deolali. It was a transit hospital where they waited to be sent back to the UK. There they caught camp fever and within days became deranged and went out of their minds. The locals called it tap fever.

I got on well with Hugh's father, who was a mentor to many. He had been through two world wars, was twice wounded on the Somme in the first war and commanded a battalion of men in Burma protecting India from invasion by the Japanese in the second. At the end of his days, he became a target for the finger-pointing wokes in his own country who had never visited India.

He was an honourable man. I wish we had talked more often and that I had listened more closely to what he had witnessed.

Once I allow my mind to doze off, that will be the end. Without its determination, I could not get out of bed, dress and wash and go up and downstairs.

I still have faith but I no longer believe in anything. I switched off the computer and turned in, bolted the back door, made myself a Horlicks and swallowed four Night Nurses, hoping for a good sleep.

Just as my eyes closed, the phone rang. It took me some time to realise that it was Harry because his voice distorted by distance.

'Hi, Gran, how are you?'

'Fine.' But of course I wasn't and he knew it. 'How is Abrinet? Her time must be near. And Sen?' I question the wisdom of bringing children into a world where they will witness such suffering; that takes not only faith but belief.

'Abrinet's fine, working as hard as ever, and Sen is a delight and looking forward to having a sibling. You would be proud of him, Gran darling.'

'One day soon I hope to see him and meet Abrinet.'

'Abrinet, Sen and I may be coming over to the UK later in the year, leaving the little he or she with Abrinet's mum. The breastfeeding should have finished by the autumn.'

'Oh, how lovely, Harry darling! In the meantime, big kisses to all and a big hug to Sentanu. God bless.'

It is difficult trying to hold onto life when your body feels weary and your mind is anxious to give up the ghost. I dragged myself downstairs to write a few words on the computer and record the conversation with Harry. I don't really know why I am doing this but it has become more necessary than spending a penny. I doubt whether anyone will bother to rea

CHAPTER 17

Connor did not want the plane to land. The magic of being above the clouds for the first time in his life – he could have stayed up there for ever. He was on Nan's magic carpet and had no wish to return to earth with all its problems.

The air stewardess was marshalling everyone for the descent. She reminded Connor of Miss. As he reached the front of the queue to disembark, he felt an overwhelming desire to kiss her but then a blast of hot air from outside the plane hit him and it was as though he were standing in front of Gloria's eye-level oven and she had opened the door unexpectedly to see how the roast was doing.

He said a quick thank you and walked down the steps onto the sand-covered tarmac, into a temperature he had never experienced before, into a no-man's land of uncertainty, crowds in foreign dress speaking in confusing tongues.

In his second letter to Harry, he had said he was coming but had received no reply. He was holding the mobile phone number that Harry had scribbled beneath his signature as he walked into the area which said 'Arrivals' in English.

Almost immediately his attention was caught by a small dark man in Arab dress smiling broadly and waving a piece of cardboard. He looked more closely and saw it was a handmade placard on which was written in capital letters 'CONER'. He waved back, smiled, walked over to him and shook his hand.

'Please, sir,' the man said. 'Follow me, sir.'

Never in his wildest dreams had Connor ever imagined that one day someone might call him sir. He would no longer be needing his yellow fluorescent jacket.

***

Harry clicked onto Aljazeera to get the local weather forecast. His Bob Dylan CD had warped in the desert heat months ago and he needed a weatherman to tell him which way the desert wind was blowing.

He called out to Connor, who was snatching a few moments' rest in the adjoining tent. 'It's going to be another scorcher. Better check the water taps, make sure the children haven't left them running. I have a day's surgery ahead. I'm hoping the aid convoy will make it today – it's already three days late.'

Connor, awaking from the half-sleep of exhaustion when dreams become nightmares, called back, 'Will do.' He tried to shake last night's dream from his head, but it wouldn't go away. Had it been a dream, or had he drifted off leaving his radio on tuned to the BBC news and his subconscious had absorbed the information that the toddler daughter of Megan and the other Harry had signed a contract with some film company for twenty million pounds? The child was being hailed as the new Shirley Temple.

Connor got up. He was still wearing yesterday's clothes. The usual day lay ahead, trying to help children forget what they had witnessed. The bombs had stopped but the population in the camps had grown.

Harry joined him, holding a package. 'I found this amongst some of the stuff I rescued from my grandmother's home the day we met.'

Connor remembered that day well; it had been the turning point in his life

Harry put the package on the small camp table and added, 'It's addressed to my grandfather from some Japanese bloke. It's never been opened – feels like a book. When you have a moment, take a look.'

'Yes, I will. But I must tell you about this stupid dream I had,' and he recited the Megan and Harry encounter.

'I wouldn't be surprised if it were true, such is the imbalance in the world. I'm surprised you have heard of Shirley Temple. She was a bit before our time.'

'My Nan used to talk about her. She used to sing some of her songs – "On the Good Ship Lollipop".

'I think you've had too much sun.'

When Harry had gone, Connor opened the package. It was a book about the building of the Burma–Thailand Railway between 1942 and 1943. He immediately recognised the author's first name, Kazuo. Amongst his old biddy's outpourings, she had written about their meeting.

He opened the book and read the handwritten inscription inside: *Dedicated to Hugh Lancaster.* He turned to the last page of the book, a thing Miss had said you must never do when reading a novel for it jaundiced your opinion of what the author was trying to tell you. Connor felt this did not apply to him as he never read books, and this did not appear to be a novel like the ones that Gloria read.

The final page was a postscript. One of the Japanese officers who had supervised the construction of the railway had written a letter after he was sentenced to death for war crimes.

It was a letter to his mother describing his love for her as being as deep as the ocean and as high as the highest mountain.

Miss would have described it as lyrical. The writer thanked his parents for their love and apologised for having to end his life without repaying them. He told his mother to take care of herself, adding that he had tried all his life to do what he was told, to obey authority and be patriotic. 'Now I shall obey Heaven's will,' he wrote.

Connor thought it the most beautiful letter, and he wondered at the young man's calmness in the face of death. He had showed no fear, only acceptance.

Connor sat quietly; never in his life had he felt such emotion and sadness. He buried his head in his hands and thought about the futility of it all, unaware that he was being watched. When he finally lifted his head he saw, standing within the open flap of the tent and silhouetted against the beauty of the rising sun, a small, naked, skeletal child, its eyes and belly enlarged and its head shrunken by malnutrition.

They stared at one another before he lifted his hand and beckoned. They stared at one another, he stretched out his hand and smiled and saw an answering flicker. The child was so emaciated that it was difficult at first to tell its age or sex, but he saw that it was a little girl. He picked her up, hardly daring to touch her fragile bones, and held her against him.

Nan was right: it is not easy to forgive.

www.ingramcontent.com/pod-product-compliance
Lightning Source LLC
Chambersburg PA
CBHW071200180726
48291CB00007B/2534